THE
SOUVENIR

*A Story of Faith, Redemption,
and the Gift of Life*

CHUCK CREWS

WESTBOW
PRESS®
A DIVISION OF THOMAS NELSON
& ZONDERVAN

WestBow Press books may be ordered through booksellers or by contacting:

WestBow Press
A Division of Thomas Nelson & Zondervan
1663 Liberty Drive
Bloomington, IN 47403
www.westbowpress.com
844-714-3454

ISBN: 978-1-6642-3225-9 (sc)
ISBN: 978-1-6642-3224-2 (hc)
ISBN: 978-1-6642-3226-6 (e)

Library of Congress Control Number: 2021908269

Print information available on the last page.

WestBow Press rev. date: 05/13/2021

For Virginia, Davis, Isabelle, and
the rest of my family.

For Jessica, Kathryn, and Rob.

For all organ transplant recipients and organ donors.

For everyone waiting for an organ transplant.

THANK YOU

I wish to thank the following people
for reading this story and providing
advice, input and encouragement.

Pam Jackson, my English teacher from high
school. She was and is inspirational. Her positive
feedback encouraged me to finish this story.

My good friends, Tony Bradley, Rusty Bodenhamer,
Carol Carter Godfrey, Carol Warfford, Tammy
Pokora, and Rob Pokora, who read *The Souvenir*
and gave their opinions and insights.

1
LAKE PLACID

The spectators clad in red, white, and blue counted down the last ten seconds, fanatically cheering the twenty young men about to pull off an upset for the ages. As the clock reached triple zeros, the dismantling of the world's greatest hockey team was complete. The final score—USA 4, USSR 3. It would become known as the miracle on ice. Movies would be made, books written, and the arena renamed for the US team's coach, Herb Brooks. But none of that mattered as the electrified fans savored the glorious moment. Americans throughout the country had watched the miracle unfold on their televisions, but nothing could match actually being inside the arena, hearing the deafening roars, watching twenty deliriously happy young men celebrate their accomplishment, and being a part of sports history.

The entire US Olympic hockey team piled on top of one another at one end of the ice, where goalie Jim

Craig had stopped so many Soviet shots late in the game. Players and assistant coaches hugged, screamed, and shook their fists toward the fanatical crowd. A few players heaved their hockey sticks into the stands. The team had pulled off the impossible—a 4–3 victory over the mighty Soviet Union hockey team, winners of four straight Olympic gold medals. The Soviet players stood at center ice, watching the craziness unfold. The only reason they stayed on the ice was the tradition that the teams meet at center ice to shake hands after a game. Looks of shock and disbelief covered their faces. This was a team that had beaten two National Hockey League teams in exhibition games. Just two weeks earlier, the Soviets had obliterated this same US Olympic team 10–3, but that game didn't count for anything now. The US had won the only game between these two teams that really mattered.

The celebration went on for what seemed like an eternity. Small American flags could be seen everywhere. Chants of "USA! USA! USA! USA!" echoed off the walls of the arena, as the raucous sea of red, white, and blue cheered the twenty newest American sports heroes.

Outside the arena, the streets of the small upstate New York town of Lake Placid were filled with joyous Americans, who hugged and high-fived strangers. The US team's momentous victory had made friends of all of them. They also chanted "USA! USA!

USA! USA!"—a chant that could be heard in towns throughout the country. Americans united to celebrate the defeat of their Cold War enemy.

Ricky Matthews and Jack Hodges were among the fans lucky enough to personally witness one of the greatest upsets in sports history. Two teenagers from a small town in south Georgia, Ricky and Jack had made an improbable trip to see this game and reveled in the moment. They chanted, yelled, screamed, cheered, and high-fived each other and all the fans near them. Their voices were practically gone—done in by sixty minutes of edge-of-your-seat, get-on-your-feet hockey and the wild scene that followed the expiration of the clock. When they exited the arena, too emotionally spent to stay any longer, Jack was carrying a hockey stick. It had been thrown into the stands by a US player and had fallen right into Jack's hands, a souvenir for a lifetime. As they walked out, Jack and Ricky were still chanting in delirious unison with their new friends. "USA! USA! USA! USA!" Neither of the boys noticed what was written in Magic Marker on the back of the stick—"Matthew 16:26."

Before this day, Jack and Ricky had known practically nothing about hockey. They had never watched a game on television before the 1980 Olympics began, and they knew few of the rules. Neither of them had ever tried ice skating or any other winter sport. They had never thrown a snowball, sledded down a hill, snow skied, or built a snowman. In fact, neither of them had ever even touched snow. They were high school seniors, and the closest they had been to snow was watching it fall outside their classroom window during geometry class in ninth grade. It was the first snow in south Georgia in over twenty years, and all they could do was watch it fall. The vice principal had forbidden students from leaving class under a threat of suspension. When the bell rang for the end of class, the students all had dashed to the doors, but outside they had found no evidence of snow except damp grass and dirt where snowflakes had fallen and quickly melted. If you had not actually seen the snow falling, you would have thought it had only rained. The sky cleared, and the next snow in Woodberry wouldn't fall for another forty years.

Like the rest of the country, Ricky and Jack had gotten caught up in the excitement of the hockey team's success. In the early rounds of the Olympics, the US team had captured the hearts of the nation with their inspired play and their ability to come from behind. They had pulled out a tie with a late goal against Sweden and had soundly beaten Czechoslovakia, a team everyone had expected to defeat the US team easily. Americans everywhere had started cheering for this group of unknown young men playing a mostly unknown sport. Ricky and Jack were among them. The game against the Soviets would be on a Friday, and Ricky was the one who had initially hatched the plan for them to drive to Lake Placid to see it. Two other classmates had been part of the plan, but both had backed out, fearing the trouble they would face for skipping town, skipping school, and generally ignoring what they all knew their parents would think of driving twenty-four hours north to watch a hockey game.

After leaving the arena, Ricky and Jack got something to eat and then roamed around Lake Placid until after midnight, basking in the excitement and pride over the big victory. No one wanted to leave the party. As far as the eye could see, fans dressed in red, white, and blue waved American flags and celebrated the win, smiling from ear to ear and occasionally breaking out in chant. It didn't seem to get old. You would have thought the US had already secured the gold medal, but that was not the case. They still needed to beat the Finland team on Sunday. No one seemed to care. On this special Friday night, all that mattered was that the upstart US hockey team, made up of twenty amateur athletes, had beaten the Soviets, the best hockey team in the world.

The US would go on to win gold on Sunday, coming from behind to defeat Finland 4–2, but Ricky and Jack would be far from Lake Placid by then. On the Saturday morning after the US–Soviet game, they started the long drive home. They had twenty-four hours of driving to relive the miracle they had witnessed, to contemplate the attention and envy they would get from their friends, and on the downside, to worry about what their parents would do to them for this insane stunt. The two teens had gotten a wild hair and just taken off to Lake Placid. They had heard there might be tickets available for the game and had decided to take the chance—two days of hooky from school, a small fortune spent, and not much to show for it except a short time to brag, some great memories, and a hockey stick, which would be worthless in south Georgia, where football was king and ice skating was as popular as Richard Nixon after the Watergate scandal. They expected their punishment to be severe.

2

FOR LOVE OF THE GAMES

When it came to sports, the students at Webb County High School never had much to cheer about. Most of their teams piled up losing season after losing season. Only the baseball team seemed able to win more than it lost, but it didn't have many championships to show for it, except winning the regional title a few times. No Webb County High team had ever won a state championship. Things had changed at WCHS during Jack's freshman year, at least in football. The Pirates were 8–2 in the regular season and qualified for the regional championship game. On the way, the Pirates managed to beat their cross-town rival, Woodberry High, for the first time ever, winning 17–14 on a last-minute field goal. No one could have predicted what would happen when the Pirates traveled to Douglas to play Catawba High for the regional title. The Trojans were undefeated and had dominated their opponents all season, including a lopsided win over Webb.

As expected, Catawba dominated the first half, scoring with less than a minute to go, to lead 20–7. The extra point was wide, but it likely wouldn't matter. Most fans on both sides of the stadium expected more of the same in the second half. The winner of the game would advance to the state playoffs. During halftime, Jack and his good friend Paul were chanting, "Where are we going? Where are we going? Straight to state!" Anyone around them who didn't know them would have thought some Catawba fans had wandered over to the visitors' bleachers. But Jack and Paul had experience with underdogs overachieving on the field. They had played youth football together for Bellview Elementary School. It was a small school with few athletes to make up a football team. The better players had to play on offense and defense every play of every game. However, in their last season they had managed two ties against heavily favored teams, both with enough players to have two separate squads for offense and defense. The Bellview players had celebrated both games as if they were wins. In one of those games, Jack had scored his only touchdown ever in organized football, when a blocked punt bounced conveniently into his hands and he dashed forty-five yards to the end zone.

At halftime of the Catawba game, Coach Bill Beckwith told his team, "Men, when they missed that extra point, they gave us the game." In the second half, the Pirates looked like a different team. They shut down the mighty Trojans and won 21–20. It was one of the biggest upsets in Georgia high school football history. The next week, the Pirates won their first-ever state playoff game. In the state semifinals, Webb ran into a tough team from Atlanta. The eventual state champions ended the Pirates' unexpected playoff run that night, Jack and his friends were left looking forward to more sports successes to cheer in the future.

The next football season ended up being a big disappointment for the Pirates fans. After nine games, the team was undefeated and ranked number one in the state when they played Woodberry to close the regular season. Because of the playoff brackets, the teams would play each other two weeks in a row—the first week for pride, the second for the regional title and a berth in the state playoffs. Going into the first game, Woodberry was also 9–0 and ranked number two. The Seminoles beat the Pirates two weeks in a row and went on to a perfect 14–0 season and the Class AAA state championship. The basketball season was equally disappointing. The boys' team went into the regional tournament with a 20–3 record and high hopes of qualifying for the state tournament for the first time in many years. They only had to win their regional semifinal game against Polk County. Instead, they ran into Jonathan Perry, a highly regarded player who would make his way to an NCAA Division I basketball program and a national championship team.

After college graduation, he would play defensive end in the National Football League. Needless to say, he was big, strong, and fast. Big Jon, as he was known, dominated the game, and the Pirates' season ended prematurely.

In Jack's junior year, Webb County's football team again found themselves in the state playoffs following an exciting overtime win in the regional semifinals and a dominating performance in the regional title game. In that regional semifinal, quarterback Timmy Johnson hit future Georgia Tech Yellow Jacket Mark Reynolds for a fifty-seven-yard touchdown pass with less than a minute to go to pull victory from the jaws of defeat. The Pirates won their first-round playoff game easily but then faced another tough opponent from Atlanta. The Pirates again lost to the eventual state champs.

The strength of the Pirates team graduated, and the team was mediocre in Jack's senior year, performing more like Pirate fans had been accustomed to for many years. The team went 5–5 and missed the playoffs when they lost the last game of the season to Catawba High. That 1979 team did manage to do one thing, though. In their last three years of high school, Jack and his classmates had never watched the Pirates lose a football game on the road. That streak almost ended at Polk County. The Pirates trailed by three touchdowns at halftime and looked completely outmanned. In the locker room, the head coach gave an "inspirational" speech to fire the team up for the second half. It wasn't a speech you will find quoted anywhere or made by a coach in some Hollywood movie. The coach, who normally addressed the team as men, said, "Boys, I'm embarrassed to be the coach of this team right now." The Pirates took the field determined to redeem themselves. They scored with less than two minutes to go, succeeded on a two-point conversion, and won 22–21. The amazing road winning streak survived the 1979 season.

Jack had managed to attend many of those away games. For most out-of-town games, the students could ride a pep bus to the game for a couple of dollars. The trip made on a regular yellow school bus was not luxurious, a smooth ride, or even moderately comfortable, but the students had fun. On the way to games, they would sing, chant, and cheer. A favorite song was "We Will Rock You" by Queen. The students would sing, "We will, we will, rock you, rock you" while stamping their feet and clapping their hands to the familiar *thump*, *thump*, *clap* beat. The ride home would not have been fun if the Pirates had lost, but Jack never experienced that sad trip. The Pirates always won on the road in the 1977, 1978, and 1979 seasons. It was a rather amazing accomplishment since, as sports fans know, the home-field advantage can be so difficult to overcome.

3

BACK TO REALITY

The rise and fall of Pirates football in their four years of high school played a part in Ricky and Jack's decision to make the road trip to Lake Placid. Like many Americans, they loved pulling for the underdog, and witnessing such a huge upset by the US team had been worth the trip. But their wild hair wasn't driven just by their sports fanaticism. The teens had grown up during the Cold War with the Russians, and the Soviet Union was considered the evil empire. The Russians had increased world tensions in 1979 by invading Afghanistan, a country few Americans had ever heard of, in what was seen as an attempt to spread communism. There were also other world conflicts at the time. Over fifty Americans were being held hostage in Iran, having been captured in 1979; they would eventually be released in 1981 after 444 days of captivity. The oil embargo had created gas shortages in the US and rising gas prices. At one point, President Jimmy Carter had threatened a US boycott of the 1980 Summer Olympics in Moscow, a threat that became a reality. In response, the Soviets had threatened to skip the Lake Placid games. The Soviet hockey team probably wished they had.

Several other events also had shaped the lives of the seniors at WCHS during their first eighteen years. Though they were too young to remember, President John F. Kennedy had been assassinated when they were still babies, a death that had made a great impact on many of the adults in their lives. Two more assassinations, of Robert F. Kennedy and Martin Luther King, had occurred when they were six years old. The Vietnam War had raged from their birth until their teens and ended in embarrassment for the United States. The country was very divided over the war, and much unrest had been caused by it, with protests and tragedies like the one at Kent State University, where four people were shot and killed by National Guard soldiers during a peace rally. In the end, over 55,000 Americans died in the Vietnam War, and many saw those deaths as a waste. There was also the Watergate scandal, which had culminated in the resignation of President Richard M. Nixon. On a more positive note, Ricky, Jack, and their classmates had also witnessed history on July 20, 1969, when Neil Armstrong stepped out of the

Apollo 11 lunar module and became the first man to walk on the moon.

On the way to Lake Placid, the two of them had been too excited about their adventure to worry about the consequences—typical teens. They had been focused on the game, whether they could get tickets, and the fun they would have on the trip. During their drive home, the mood changed. Ricky and Jack were still giddy from their experience, but as they got closer to home, fear started to overcome them.

"What do you think Bob will do to you when you get home?" Jack asked Ricky, whose father was well known for his temper and sometimes harsh treatment of his children for even minor transgressions.

"I don't know. You may have to visit me in the hospital," Ricky joked. They both laughed uneasily. Then Ricky continued, "Bob will probably just put me on restriction and hard labor." Ricky always referred to his father by his first name, except when his dad was within earshot.

"Yeah, my guess is I won't get to do much except go to school for a while. That and the Holiday Inn." Jack was a desk clerk at the motel on Saturday and Sunday nights.

"I'm a little worried about my schoolwork," said Jack. "I've never missed a day of school before."

"Not one day?" asked Ricky incredulously.

"Nope. Not even during kindergarten."

"Man, Jack, you really are a nerd."

After a long silence, Jack said to Ricky, "No matter what happens when we get home, I'm glad we did this. I'll never forget being at that game."

"Me too," said Ricky. "I didn't think anything would top going to the Masters, but this was way better. They play the Masters every year, but something like this will probably never happen again."

"Our friends will be so jealous, especially Bill and John."

"Hey, and you have the hockey stick to show off. Some of our friends might even know what it is," kidded Ricky. "Who knows, it might be worth something one day."

Jack had almost forgotten about the hockey stick. The one person he thought would love it was his father, Matt.

Neither Jack nor Ricky would ever admit it to their parents, but they recognized that the punishment they ultimately received was light. Maybe it was their fear of the worst that made it seem that way. Both were grounded for a month. They both went to school, and Jack went to his job and then home. They were lucky. After all, they had left on a trip involving a twenty-four-hour drive without their parents' knowledge or permission, calling them only after they had driven several hours from home. They had spent a lot of money, missed two full days of school, and slept in their car for the entire trip. Neither of them had even had a shower since they left home. Their parents had been worried sick. It was a parents' nightmare.

The rest of their senior year passed without much excitement. They had prom and a few parties. Ricky went on a cruise with a group of seniors. Jack went on the official senior trip to New York City and Washington, DC. The highlights included a Broadway show, the Statue of Liberty, the Washington Monument, and laying a wreath on the Tomb of the Unknown Soldier in Arlington National Cemetery. A big thrill for Jack was meeting Walter Cronkite at a New York City restaurant. Jack was the editor of the Webb County High School newspaper, and Cronkite was *the* television news anchorman of the time. It was a memorable trip, especially for a bunch of kids from south Georgia, many of whom had never been more than 250 miles from home. After graduation, the class somewhat went their separate ways, especially Jack. Some of the graduates got jobs and stayed close to home. Some enlisted in the military and left for basic training and whatever followed. Some were going to college at the end of the summer. While many of his friends went off to colleges and universities in Georgia, Jack left in the fall for Duke University in Durham, North Carolina. Jack was bright and a great student. His missing two days of school for the

Olympic trip had been out of character for him and had caught his teachers by surprise, but it surprised none of them that he would attend an excellent academic institution.

4

MOVING ON TO GREENER PASTURES

When Jack left home for school, he took the hockey stick with him. Jack's father, Matt Hodges, had always been a huge sports fan and saw the stick as a wonderful piece of sports memorabilia to share with family and friends in the future, to remind Jack of what he had witnessed, and to help him savor the memories of witnessing one of the greatest sporting events of his day, a treasured piece of sports history.

Jack didn't see the hockey stick that way at all. It was his inspiration. He had read articles about the 1980 US hockey team. Those young men had worked hard and achieved success far greater than anyone had expected from them. They were the epitome of what could happen when people knew what they wanted and were willing to make great sacrifices to get it. To Jack, the hockey stick represented the idea that hard work and determination would make a person successful in life. Jack had never been a great athlete and would never experience tremendous success in sports. He was intelligent, though, and he knew that through hard work, he could become highly successful in business or some profession. To him, that meant making plenty of money. From that day forward, the hockey stick would inspire Jack to succeed in his career, no matter the cost.

Jack had always been an enigma of sorts. He loved sports. He loved to play. He loved to watch. He was an avid supporter of his teams. But he had never been a great athlete, and he was painfully aware that he would never be successful in any sport. Jack's fixation on sports was born of the environment in which he lived and belied his academic abilities, which were barely noticed or appreciated by the other students in his classes. In fact, those abilities were a cause for ridicule. Intelligence was not exactly celebrated at his school, and Jack tried to keep a low profile.

Teachers had recognized Jack's gifts and tried to encourage him to push the upward limits of his intellect, but he had never really embraced his academic ability. He had participated on the math team and entered into some creative writing competitions, but otherwise he had kept a low profile and mostly underachieved in the classroom. Although he had been named the

"STAR Student" for making the highest score on the Scholastic Aptitude Test, Jack was not the valedictorian or salutatorian of his class. He graduated fourth in a class of 245 seniors.

5

HIGHER EDUCATION

After arriving at Duke, Jack fully engaged his mind and let his ambitions take over his life. His focus changed from sports and a fruitless attempt to be part of the "in" crowd to achieving academically. Even though Jack loved sports, Duke was not exactly a mecca for those gifted with athletic prowess, and he didn't often go to sporting events. The school had some success on the basketball court, but most of it came after Jack left the school in 1984. While many of Jack's friends were at the University of Georgia cheering for the Bulldogs and witnessing Georgia's 1980 national championship season, Jack was hunkered down in the library. He earned his degree in four years, graduating with honors.

Jack's academic career wasn't over, though. He was accepted into the University of North Carolina School of Law in Chapel Hill. Admission was highly competitive, especially among out-of-state students, and Jack was happy he had made the cut. After returning to the Holiday Inn in Woodberry for the summer after graduating from Duke, Jack started his first year of law school in the fall of 1984.

Jack found that the stories, movies, and books about law school were not exaggerations. It was tough. The first year was known to be especially brutal. It was said that a law student should spend three hours of study for each hour in class. First-year students, or 1Ls as they were called, especially needed to spend the time. In addition to the normal first-year load—property, contracts, torts, civil procedure, criminal law, and constitutional law—1Ls also had research and writing requirements, competitions in moot court and mock trial, and recommended extracurricular reading. Moot court was typically an appellate court competition in which the competitors must write an appellate brief and also make oral arguments. The brief could support either side of the case, but each student must be prepared to argue both sides. Mock trial was trial work, including opening statements, witness examinations, cross-examinations, and closing arguments. As an advocacy exercise, the competitions included two rounds, with the students changing sides of the case for each round. It went without saying that the first year was quite challenging.

The most stressful time of law school was exam period. The exam score accounted for the entire grade in a class. A student could be brilliant in one-on-one exchanges with professors, all of whom used the Socratic method. But no matter how impressed a professor was with a student in class, it was only the final written exam that mattered. Exams were written anonymously, and the professor did not know which student's paper was being graded.

The first year was so rigorous that many students formed study groups. They didn't really study together, though. Each person was responsible for creating a course outline to share with the group, with one person in the study group assigned to each of the semester's courses. To most 1Ls it was the only way to assure themselves the study materials they needed. Jack decided to go it alone. He had always been a team player when it came to sports, but academics were a different story. He was an academic loner—resulting from a mix of mistrust of others and an arrogant belief that he was better off not relying on lesser minds. When first-semester grades were released, Jack's belief that he should work alone was strengthened. He was ranked ninth in the class of 150 students.

In law school, class rank, not grade point average, was the measure of academic success. By the end of the year, Jack had moved up to eighth. His achievement placed Jack on the law review, an elite organization made up of the top 10 percent of the class. In addition to classroom success, Jack exceeded in extracurriculars too. He was runner-up in the first-year moot court competition, earning him a spot on the Moot Court Board. In mock trial, he made the semifinals. His future seemed secure, especially when a large Atlanta law firm offered him a summer internship. Jack was one of only eighteen first-year students to land a paid summer internship at a law firm.

The second year of law school was difficult academically, but less hectic and stressful than first year. At North Carolina, evidence, criminal procedure, and the second part of constitutional law were the only required classes. Students could fill the rest of their schedule with elective courses. Jack loaded up on classes geared toward litigation and business law. He performed well, but those classes attracted the brighter students. For each class, the professor graded the students' exams on a bell curve, so the students in a class were compared to each other, not necessarily to all the students in the entire second-year class. There was a ranking of the students within each class, and then those rankings were translated into an overall grade and class rank. Therefore, a student could perform better in a class with students who were not as bright. This grading method impacted Jack slightly during the second year. His overall rank dropped from eighth to twelfth. He wasn't happy, but jobs for the summer following second year were filled during the fall semester of the second year. Before any grades were released for second-year classes, Jack already had a summer internship lined up with Brooks & Duncan, an Atlanta-based firm with offices throughout the country and even some overseas.

The partners at Brooks & Duncan were impressed with Jack's intellect, work ethic, and legal acumen. Jack had become more of a loner and didn't seem to care about bonding with his fellow interns. In Jack's mind, the culture at the firm rewarded long days, billable hours, and positive results. Jack fit that mold and was offered a permanent position after law school graduation.

The third year of law school was by far the easiest. Most students already had jobs lined up and were just finishing out the year to get their *juris doctorate*. For class rank, it was difficult to move the needle much after you had so many credit hours. Jack used the complacency of others to work a little harder, gain a little ground, and achieve his goal—a top-ten finish overall.

Jack shrugged off the attention from his family about his graduating with honors. In fact, he didn't invite anyone except his parents to graduation. Though it wasn't true, he told his family there were limited seats. After graduation, all of the new graduates began preparing for the bar exam. For a student of Jack's caliber, the bar was a piece of cake, and he passed easily. He heard that a few of his classmates had failed their state's bar exam, and he marveled at how they could have performed so poorly. In the end, he didn't care. Their failure had no impact on his life or career. Jack had become friends with other elite students in the class, and any failure by the lower end was not his problem.

6

LEARNING THE ROPES
OF PRACTICING LAW

In September after his law school graduation, Jack started his new position and settled right into the work routine at Brooks & Duncan. As in all large firms, associates at Brooks & Duncan were expected to work long days to make the billable-hour requirements set by the firm. A Brooks associate was expected to bill 2,200 hours annually. That was a lofty sum considering the normal work year was 2,000 hours. Some associates struggled to make billing goals, but not Jack. He quickly learned how to play the hour-billing game.

The firm, like many others, billed in quarter-hour increments. Take a five-minute phone call from a client or an opposing attorney—bill for fifteen minutes. Read a letter relevant to a case, and bill that two minutes as a quarter hour. Do an hour of research on an issue germane to two cases you are working, and bill each client for an hour. To some, these practices seemed immoral and unethical. To Jack and many other firm partners and associates, it was the way to survive and thrive in the firm's culture.

Jack's office was much like the offices of all associate attorneys, but it also featured the hockey stick. Jack loved it when people asked about the stick. He would tell them the story of being at the Olympics and witnessing the upset by the US over the Soviets. More than anything, though, the stick continued to provide Jack the motivation to succeed. Over the years since 1980, Jack had read articles about the members of the US hockey team. The team had been a hodgepodge of talented players, but not necessarily the best ones available. They had gelled as a team, and much of their success could be traced to Herb Brooks, the unmerciful coach who had told the team that no one had ever worked hard enough to beat the Soviets. He had promised them they would work hard enough, and he'd kept his word. The hockey stick was a constant reminder that Jack needed to outwork his peers to achieve the success he desired.

Jack became known as a billing machine. In his first year as an associate, he billed over 2,500 hours to clients. In his first three years, he never fell below 2,400 hours per year. The quality of his legal work, especially his research and writing skills, was among the best of all the firm's associates with less than five year's experience. He was a rising star. He worked in the litigation section of the firm, representing various clients in legal disputes. In most cases, the firm represented defendants, such as insurance companies, hospitals and doctors, and large corporations. Jack worked mostly on complex business litigation cases. It was his involvement in one of the firm's biggest corporate cases during his first year that helped solidify his place among the firm's elite.

7

CAREER ON THE RISE

For three years prior to Jack's arrival at Brooks, the firm had represented a large construction corporation, Walker Construction Inc., in a civil RICO case. RICO stood for the Racketeering Influenced and Corrupt Organizations Act, a federal statute designed primarily to fight organized crime. However, many defendants had been caught up in civil cases because of allegedly criminal behavior by the company's officers. Unlike in most cases, Brooks represented the plaintiff in this matter. The basic allegation was that the defendant corporation had been paying the plaintiff's president kickbacks in exchange for favorable treatment on contracts. The defendant corporation would pad its bid on jobs and always seemed to be awarded contracts even though the bids were considerably higher than bids from other firms.

The defendant corporation was represented by another large Atlanta firm. The lead counsel for the defendant firm had been belligerent and had flatly denied all allegations for three years. He threatened Brooks with sanctions for abuse of the legal process and generally stonewalled any progress on the case. The attorneys at Adams & Wright, the defense firm, accused all the Brooks lawyers of unethical behavior and called the litigation specious.

Jack played a pivotal role in breaking the case wide open. For over a year, Brooks had held over twenty boxes of documents they had received through the legal discovery process, but no one had really reviewed the contents. Jack was curious about what information the boxes contained. He glanced through them and saw various financial records. He asked Winston Smith, the lead counsel on the case for Brooks, if he could spend some time digging through the files.

"I've always heard the best way to uncover the truth is to follow the trail of money," Jack said to Winston.

"Have at it," replied Winston. "But we can't justify you billing your time on this unless you find something. The CFO at Walker would have a cow."

Jack spent a week digging through files, reading documents, and trying to figure out whether the documents really meant anything. There were corporate filings, tax returns, stockholder agreements, other various papers, and some bank statements for about two dozen companies. After a week, Jack was about ready to give up. Then he found something intriguing. Buried in an obscure letter about some random topic, Jack found the name Bobby Walker, the president of the plaintiff corporation. Jack again remembered a line spoken by the person known as Deep Throat, played by Hal Holbrook, in the movie *All the President's Men*, about the Watergate scandal that led to President Nixon's resignation: "Follow the money."

Jack dug into the bank statements. After two more weeks of reading documents, researching various companies through the records division at the Georgia secretary of state's office, and doing the painstaking grunt work of developing a method for reporting his findings, Jack went to see Winston Smith. When he went into Smith's office, Jack was carrying a large spreadsheet. Finding Winston's desk covered with various court documents, letters, and other miscellaneous papers, Jack suggested they find an open conference room. Finding a clean table, Jack laid out the spreadsheet. It was actually four pieces of graphing paper taped together. On the right side was the name of the defendant corporation, Atkinson Contractors. In between were the names of all those companies from the documents in the boxes. The spreadsheet looked like a big flowchart that spread out wide from Atkinson and then narrowed back down as it reached the name of a Georgia limited liability company.

"What's this?" Winston asked.

"This," said a gleaming Jack, "is proof that Atkinson has been paying kickbacks to Walker." Jack explained, "Atkinson has been using dummy companies to filter money to Bobby Walker. Atkinson would pay one of about a dozen companies for phony invoices. The money would then be paid out to two or three other companies and then eventually would make its way to a limited liability company called 'Construction Consulting Associates.' That LLC was established by an attorney in Quitman, Georgia."

"So? What does that have to do with Bobby Walker?" inquired Smith.

"Francine Walker grew up in Quitman," said Jack. "The registered address of Construction Consulting Associates is her brother's house." Francine Walker was Bobby Walker's wife.

"Wow," said a surprised Winston Smith. "So Walker used his wife's family to hide what he's been doing!"

"Exactly," said Jack. "Over a five-year period I traced about $450,000 from Atkinson to this LLC."

Without another word, Smith darted out of the conference room. Soon other partners who had labored on the case for three years began to show up. Jack explained to them the complex scheme he had uncovered and showed them the documents that supported his conclusions. The evidence didn't absolutely prove Walker was dirty, but everyone thought it came close enough.

Jack drafted what was known as "requests for admission," asking Atkinson to admit the payments to Bobby Walker. The requests were very detailed, to show the defendants that the plaintiff's counsel had proof of their illegal scheme. After the requests for admission were served on the defense, the defense's lead lawyer, the fiery attorney who had done nothing but stonewall for three years, meekly asked Winston Smith for a one-on-one meeting. Two hours after the meeting started, the parties had reached a settlement.

Brooks made a fortune on the case. The firm's attorneys had billed all their time at reduced rates for three years. Then the firm received 20 percent of the $25 million settlement. Jack didn't see any of that money. All he got was a long weekend and a nice lunch. A bonus would have been nice, but Jack wasn't too disappointed. He had made a name for himself at Brooks and Duncan. His career was taking off.

8

CHOOSING A
DIFFERENT PATH

Jack had met Regina during their first year of law
school and had been immediately smitten with her.
Like Jack, she was a good student. She was on the law
review and could always be counted on by professors
to be prepared for class. Like Jack, Regina seemed
destined for an associate position at a large firm. At
least that's what Jack and other classmates thought.
She clerked with a large firm, Miller, Graves, and
Donaldson, during the summer after second year. The
firm was also in Atlanta but was somewhat smaller
than Brooks. Regina was assigned to the section of the
firm representing creditors. Regina's work impressed
the partners, and they offered her an associate's
position after graduation. Instead of accepting this
lucrative position, Regina accepted a job with a small

nonprofit organization providing legal assistance to underprivileged families.

Jack was surprised. "Regina, I don't understand this decision. Why would you accept such a low-paying job? Miller Graves offered you twice the salary you're getting."

"Jack, I didn't go to law school just to make money. I want to do some meaningful work. Last summer, most of the people I worked against were poor and just down on their luck."

"To me, most of them were deadbeats who just didn't want to pay their bills."

"It's not that simple, Jack. Many of those people just had a run of bad luck that caused their money problems. They had medical bills, cars that died, parents and kids to take care of. People don't choose to be poor, and the ones who end up homeless don't choose that either."

Regina's job was with the Georgia Legal Services Agency. The agency assisted low-income clients with credit issues, landlord–tenant problems, vehicle cases involving the state's "lemon law," and just about any other issue normally facing lower-income families. Jack was somewhat disappointed in her decision to accept the job, but it didn't affect his feelings for her. He was head-over-heels in love with Regina. They got married right after the bar exam, went on their honeymoon, and then settled into their jobs. For many years into their marriage, Jack would not understand Regina's attraction to helping people who had legal troubles created by their own poor decisions, but the work seemed to make her happy, so he let the issue go.

Whoever is generous to the poor lends to the Lord, and He will repay them for what they have done.
—Proverbs 19:17 (NIV)

For her part, Regina accepted the long hours Jack worked. She was fully aware of what Jack's life had been like when he was a kid and teenager. Jack had not grown up in a wealthy family. His parents had provided very well for the family's needs and many of the things they wanted, but they hadn't enjoyed many luxuries like some families. Regina understood Jack's ambition to become a wealthy attorney, but she was actually jealous of the family life he'd had in Woodberry. She loved her parents, and she had wanted for very little as she was growing up. However, her family was not warm like Jack's. Regina's parents had both worked, especially her father. He'd had little time for his children, and Regina had grown up wanting more attention from her dad. He had rarely attended any of Regina's events or games. She had played basketball and softball in high school. In fact, she was good enough in basketball that she was offered a scholarship at a small school in south Georgia, but she decided to attend a private school with a great reputation for academics. Regina could count the number of games her father had attended on her two hands, and she had always wished he had been there more.

Regina didn't have student loans. Her parents had been able to pay for her undergraduate and law school educations. They offered to pay off Jack's loans, but he declined. Jack was driven to succeed, and he would see it as a failure to accept that kind of help. Regina didn't worship money or care whether outsiders viewed her as wealthy and successful. Much to Regina's chagrin, Jack would become more and more concerned about outward appearances as the years passed. As he became more successful, his salary rose quickly, and he insisted they move into the "right" neighborhood. They found a new home in a gated community. It was large and luxurious and would make the right impression on any guests they might have. Of course, they rarely had guests because of the long hours Jack worked. By the end of the week, he was physically and emotionally exhausted. He often had to work on Saturdays and rarely wanted to do anything or see anyone.

Jack also withdrew from his family even more than before. He had never talked to his parents very often after he started law school. His contact with them was even less frequent now. Regina talked to them more frequently than he did. They were always pleasant and asked about Jack, his work, and when they might come to visit. Regina could tell they were hurt about the lack of contact with him, but they never actually said so.

> Honor your father and your mother, so that you may live long in the land the LORD your God is giving you.
> —Exodus 20:12 (NIV)

9

GROWING APART

For the first few years, Regina continued to tolerate the long hours and Jack's attitude about work, money, and climbing the social ladder. Jack still felt that Regina's job was beneath her and that her clients were deadbeats and losers, but he was wise enough to keep his feelings to himself. They'd had several arguments about it early in their marriage, and he had learned it was a battle he couldn't win. However, after several years of tension caused by their different attitudes about work and money, Regina and Jack's marriage started to show signs of strain. Not much was said between them about it, but the silence spoke volumes. In the past, the two of them had managed to engage in conversation that was interesting, satisfying, and most of all, frequent. After three years of eighty-hour weeks, Jack had gotten to the point where he quickly retreated into a shell when he was not working. Regina tried to break through it but became increasingly dissatisfied with their life.

"The Johnsons invited us over for dinner Saturday."

"I don't want to go over there," replied Jack. "All they talk about is their bratty kids and all the time they spend helping the less fortunate." Jack smirked as he spoke, making his disdain clear. Peter Johnson was the director of an organization that worked with homeless families, and Regina volunteered her time and legal skills to the cause. Paula Johnson was a certified public accountant with a small firm that focused on tax work for individuals and small businesses.

"Not everyone cares as much as you about making and flaunting money," said Regina.

"Well, excuse me. I didn't grow up with a silver spoon in my mouth like most of your friends," Jack said. "And I don't flaunt money."

"You don't know anything about most of my friends. The Johnsons aren't rich and don't care about being rich, just like most of my friends. Peter chose to work at the job he has because he wanted to help people and make a difference in the community."

Of course, Jack knew that the Johnsons had inherited enough money that they didn't have a house payment, which made life much easier for them financially. It allowed them the one luxury they really enjoyed—travel. Every year their family took a vacation together, and they always shared pictures from their trips.

"I don't flaunt money. Look at the Johnsons. Every time they take a trip, we hear about it endlessly and see all their pictures. They couldn't afford to do that if they had to pay for their house."

"You don't flaunt money? Really? What about that car you drive?"

Jack had bought a Mercedes-Benz with all the bells and whistles. Regina drove a Honda Civic.

"It hurts when you talk about my friends, especially when you belittle what some of them do for a living. What do you think I do all day at work?" Regina continued.

"You help a bunch of deadbeats and get paid very little to do it," Jack replied. "You could have done so much better."

"Not everyone measures success by the size of their bank account."

"That's easy for you to say. You grew up with everything you ever wanted."

This type of conversation between Regina and Jack became more frequent over time. Whenever Jack's attacks became personal, Regina would leave the room. She wanted to respond in a way that would hurt his feelings as badly as he hurt hers, but she held her tongue. The worst thing she could have told him was that she had graduated sixth in their law school class, three spots ahead of him. Jack would never know that little fact.

> You have heard that it was said, "Eye for eye, and tooth for tooth." But I tell you, do not resist an evil person. If anyone slaps you on the right cheek, turn to them the other cheek also.
> —Matthew 5:38–39 (NIV)

Jack couldn't really say he loved his work. He found the cases complex and challenging, and being able to name-drop the large Atlanta companies he represented made him feel important. But the work wasn't necessarily rewarding, except financially. Jack really loved the money he was making and would continue to make. That was the driving force for him. He started to push aside all of the things he had enjoyed so much in the past. When he looked at the hockey stick, he didn't think of the excitement of being at the hockey game or his limited past triumphs in sports or the fun he'd had as a fan of his high school sports teams or being in the high school golf team. All he thought about was how that hockey stick inspired him to succeed in his career. Hard work, determination, and dedication to your goals—the stick told him that was all it took, and nothing else mattered.

> No one can serve two masters. Either you will hate the one and love the other, or you will be devoted to the one and despise the other. You cannot serve both God and money.
> —Matthew 6:24 (NIV)

10

LEAVING BEHIND
BOYISH PASSIONS

Between the ages of ten and thirteen, Jack had managed to make two baseball all-star teams. However, his enthusiasm for sports far exceeded his abilities. He loved both professional and college football, Major League baseball, and college basketball. He was an avid Atlanta Braves fan, idolizing Hank Aaron and his journey to become baseball's home-run king. But Aaron was the only good thing about being a Braves fan. Year after year, the Braves languished among the league's worst teams and often finished near the bottom of their division. The 1982 season was an exception. The Braves opened the season with thirteen straight wins and went on to win the division. Jack was in college then and was still pulling for the Braves. After winning the division, the Braves were swept by the St. Louis Cardinals in the National League Championship series.

The Braves didn't make the playoffs again until 1991. After finishing last the year before, the Braves had a miracle season in 1991 and won the National League's western division. The Braves then won games six and seven of the NLCS in Pittsburgh with two straight shutouts to make the World Series. In the series, the Minnesota Twins won four games to three in one of the most exciting World Series ever played.

The next season proved the Braves' 1991 season was not a fluke. They won their division again for a rematch with the Pirates. In game seven, the Braves went to the bottom of the last inning trailing 2–0. After scoring one run, the Braves loaded the bases. With two outs, little-used Francisco Cabrera delivered a single to left. The tying run scored from third. Sid Bream, who had been on second, lumbered around third base and headed home. An accurate throw would have gotten the third out and sent the game to extra innings, but Barry Bonds's throw was to the first-base side of the plate. The Pirates' catcher caught the ball and lunged toward Bream, whose slide just beat the tag. Skip Carey, the Braves play-by-play radio man, made the call: "Braves win, Braves win, Braves win, Braves win, Braves win!" The Braves got a second straight trip to the World Series, which they lost to the Toronto Blue Jays.

The Braves' success was lost on Jack, who was four years into his legal career at Brooks & Duncan. That had become his passion. Actually, it was more of an obsession. He didn't necessarily have passion for the work he was doing. He was obsessed with partnership, wealth, and prestige. He would sometimes think about little league baseball, his Monday afternoon golf games with his dad, going to high school football games during those winning years at WCHS, and his trip to Lake Placid. But those memories no longer brought any joy or even a smile to his face. Jack worked long hours in a highly stressful environment. At the end of the day, all he wanted to do was go home to a quiet evening.

Jack's loss of passion for sports caused him to push his family further away. Sports was the one thing Jack had in common with his dad. When Jack was growing up, they were always playing sports, watching sports, or talking about sports. Jack never grasped what that bond could do for a father and son. He also missed that the bond would have extended beyond athletics if he had just reached out to Matt more often. Matt wasn't highly educated, but he was bright and would have appreciated conversations with Jack about the law and his work. It didn't occur to Jack that Matt would be even remotely interested in what he was doing.

11

PARTNERSHIP, A BETTER LIFE, AND A BABY

In 1995, Jack was named a partner at Brooks & Duncan. His legal career and marriage had coexisted for eight years. Jack was drawn to his work not because he loved it, but because the money he made was intoxicating. In reality, the firm was like a mistress for Jack, from whom he just couldn't stay away even when Regina complained about missed parties, canceled weekend trips, and cold dinners sitting on the table at night. With the achievement of partner, Jack promised that things would get better. They did, for about six months.

During that time, Jack spent more time with Regina and was more like the man she had fallen in love with during law school. They went out to dinner, hosted two parties, went on their first real vacation since their honeymoon to Williamsburg, and had quiet dinners together in the evenings, at a normal time. Around November, Regina started being sick in the mornings. She went to an obstetrician and confirmed her suspicion. She was pregnant, due in June 1996.

Over the next few months, Regina always had that motherly glow about her. It was obvious that she was excited about her pending role as a mother. On the other hand, it didn't take Jack long to fall back into the same old routine—go to work early, stay late, bill seemingly countless hours, and take home a big paycheck. He didn't seem excited that he was going to be a father. His role as he saw it was to make as much money as possible to provide for the family's needs.

Regina spent her alone time preparing for the baby's arrival. She painted the room that would be used as the nursery, shopped for baby furniture, bought other baby items, and joined a group of expectant mothers at her church. They were supportive of each other and spent time socializing and discussing their pending motherhood.

Regina had enjoyed her time working as an attorney with underprivileged families. It gave her a great deal of joy to assist families working with debt issues, landlord problems, and a myriad of other legal issues encountered by the poor. Jack had continued to mostly see her clients as ne'er-do-wells who were the real cause of their own problems. He had long ago learned to never talk to her about her clients but instead just listened and offered no opinions. Regina finally had quit discussing her work around Jack. Two months before the baby was to be born, Regina left her job to be a stay-at-home mom.

12

CHURCH IS NOT FOR JACK

Regina got more involved in her church. It was *her* church. Jack never attended. Sunday morning was his time to sleep in and relax. After he woke up on Sunday, he would read the paper, drink coffee, and usually end up working for an hour or two. Truth be told, he didn't believe the church could do anything meaningful for him. He didn't see the value of volunteering your time, helping others, or even going to worship and studying the Bible. He thought money was the answer to any problem. He told Regina to write checks for the causes she was supporting, but he didn't want to be actually involved in any of the church's work. He resisted all efforts by Regina, the pastor, and other church members to get him to attend worship services or do anything else with the church.

"Why won't you go to church with me, Jack?"

"My parents always made me go," said Jack. "I just don't care about being there now. What's the point?

Don't you spend enough time as it is doing for others? That's all churches seem to want to do."

"That's not the only reason to be there. The best hours I have every week are the ones right after I've been to worship services."

"What?"

"When I was a kid, we went to church, but my family never talked about God, prayed, or did anything else that you would think of as religious. I never knew how worshipping could make you feel until I really did it."

"Don't tell me you buy into all that 'inner joy from having a relationship with God' junk."

"Jack, we never really talked about these things when we were at UNC, but hearing about your family, I assumed you would want to be involved in church after school was over."

"Well, I don't. But I don't mind if you want it."

Many young parents decide to begin attending church after having a child. The reasons vary. Many attended church while growing up, stopped going to church in their young adult years, and begin to see the light when children are in the picture. Whatever the reason, for many parents a church family provides support, regular contact with other adults at similar stages in life, and friends for the children. Many such families grow into faithful church members and servants of God. Jack had no intention of gong to church even after their child was born.

When William was born in June, Jack's parents visited for a weekend to see their grandson and to help get the new parents settled into the new routine of having an infant in the house. Jack was glad for the help but wasn't exactly sad when they left. They lived only five hours away, but Jack rarely saw them. It wouldn't be accurate to say he was estranged from his family, but Jack intentionally kept them at a distance. His brother Tom and sister Carol were living proof of how different children growing up in the same household could be.

Carol was a social worker married to a city police officer in their small hometown. The couple lived in an older home, drove cheap cars, and had no savings to speak of. With three teenage children, they were barely making ends meet. Carol had a college degree, but her ambitions had never included making money. She had married her high school sweetheart and never left Woodberry, having gone to a junior college in town for two years before commuting to get her bachelor's degree. Carol worked for the Department of Social Services, ensuring that children were not abused by their parents. To many, it was a noble job, but it didn't match Jack's definition of success. Her husband had an associate's degree in criminal justice and had been a cop since he was twenty years old. He regularly patrolled a neighborhood riddled with drug use and crime. He wasn't exactly popular with the criminal element of the neighborhood, but most of the people there, who were law-abiding citizens just trying to raise their children in a tough place, understood how vital Bob was to their neighborhood and had immense respect for him.

Tom was equally unsuccessful in Jack's eyes. He was an officer at a small local bank. To Jack, it was a small-town bank working with small-town people, giving Tom no real hope of ever building the kind of wealth that Jack saw as defining success. What Jack didn't know about Tom was that he was the local equivalent of George Bailey from the movie *It's a Wonderful Life*. He had helped hundreds of families buy homes, start small businesses, and send their children to college. He had provided financing for churches to build new sanctuaries and youth centers. He worked with local nonprofit groups to stretch their dollars and provide a higher level of care for the beneficiaries of the organizations. Everyone in town loved Tom, and he was highly respected. Tom's wife was an elementary school teacher loved by her second-grade students and their parents.

No, neither of Jack's siblings were successful in his eyes. They were "small-town" with all the negative connotations that phrase conjured. Jack, on the other hand, was a huge success. He was a partner in a prestigious law firm in the South's largest city, working with the top brass of some of the world's best-known corporations. He figured he made more money than his sister, his brother, and their spouses combined.

> The closer a husband and wife get to God, the closer they get to each other. The farther away they get from God, the farther they get from each other.
>
> —Author unknown

13

FUN AND MEDIOCRITY
ON THE PLAYING FIELDS

Jack's father worked at a railroad yard in their
hometown. For as long as Jack could remember, his
dad had worked the graveyard shift, 11:00 p.m. to 7:00
a.m. It paid more than the day shift and also meant
he slept during the day. Matt's routine was to leave
work at seven, go straight home to see his children
before they left for school, and then go straight to
bed to sleep all day. He was usually up when everyone
returned from school. He would spend the evening
with the family, including eating dinner, and then
leave for work around 10:30 p.m. Frequently, instead
of enjoying a quiet evening at home, he would attend
the children's various activities. During basketball
season, Matt was involved with the boys' teams as an
assistant coach. He would later become a head coach,
a gig he would do the rest of his life.

On Mondays, Matt would pick the boys up from school and take them to a local par-3 golf course, where they would play nine holes. It was a well-maintained course owned by a local corporation. The company had built the course for its employees but had opened it to the public after a few years. Tom, who was three years older than Jack, was an above-average golfer. Jack was not as good, but he really enjoyed the game, more than Tom. He played on the high school golf team and had a lot of fun doing it. Ricky, who would end up making the journey to Lake Placid with Jack, was also on the team. Ricky was a much better golfer than Jack, as were all the team members, but they all enjoyed the camaraderie of the team. They especially liked going to away golf matches. The team would usually get out of school early and travel to matches by mini-bus. They would play the match on courses much nicer than they had at home and then drive home, picking up fast food on the way. Jack was the sixth player on the six-person team, and his only real goal was to break 90 in one match.

Ricky was the number three player on the team, so he usually didn't play with Jack in matches. For one particular match, Ricky asked the coach to pair him with Jack. On the first tee, Ricky told Jack, "You're going to break 90 today." He helped Jack throughout the match, giving him advice on clubs to hit and shots to play, helping him read putts, and generally keeping

Jack focused on the match. It worked. Jack shot 40 on the front nine, just four over par. It was Jack's best-ever score on nine holes. Jack didn't play as well on the back, shooting 46. But it was done, a score of 86. It was the first and only time Jack shot under 90 in a high school match. When Jack left for college, his golf clubs were left in the family garage to gather dust.

Jack also played basketball. During his younger years, he played in the recreation league, with his dad as assistant coach. No matter the time for a practice or a game, Matt was always there. He had a way with children. They didn't realize they were learning the game and also some life lessons thrown in because they were having so much fun. Matt's players loved him, and it showed. Many teams had one kid who was better than the rest, and that kid tried to do it all. Not on Matt's teams. The kids showed up at practice and learned to play like a team. As a consequence, they won—a lot. During warm-ups for a game, the opposing team probably watched their skills and thought Matt's team could be beaten easily. But when the game started, the teamwork on offense and defense made the sum of the team much greater than its parts. Of course, some teams were just too skilled for them, but if the teams had equal abilities, Matt's teams would win every time.

Jack benefited from his dad's basketball tutelage. As a member of the junior varsity team in tenth grade,

Jack played point guard. He wasn't as good as the starter. He couldn't handle the ball as well or shoot as well. One-on-one, he wasn't as good on defense. But the coach loved Jack for his dedication, hustle, and teamwork. Jack gave it his all from the start of practice to the end. He pushed the other players to do the same. As a result, he got more playing time than his skills would have dictated. Even though he wasn't as good as Ronny, the starting point guard, the team had a higher energy level when Jack was on the court. They played more cohesively. It was the best year of high school basketball that Jack would have. As always, Ricky was there too. He was a better player than Jack and had some great games on offense, scoring a season-high twenty-four points in one game.

Near the end of Jack's sophomore year, the varsity coach held tryouts for the next season's varsity team. As always, Jack gave it his all. At the end of the two weeks, the team played an intra-squad game on Friday night. Jack and Ronny were matched against each other as point guards. During the game, two things were obvious—Ronny had better basketball skills, and his team was somewhat stacked with the better players. Everyone expected Ronny's team, dressed in red, to beat the white team easily. The game didn't go as they predicted. The teamwork displayed by the white kept the game close. Every time the red team would try to pull away, the white players would claw back into the game. The teams were never separated by more than seven points. With thirty seconds left, the red team had the ball with the score tied. The red tried to run a play, but each player seemed to want to be the hero. With four seconds left, Ronny got trapped near mid-court and threw an errant pass that went out of bounds. Jack then did something no one had done during the entire game. He called time-out.

The two teams had no coaches, so Jack pulled his team into a huddle, and they developed a play. Everyone gathered around mid-court in a staggered line down the half-court line. When the referee gave Jack the ball, he slapped it to set the play in motion. John and Michael set a pick for Ricky, who broke toward the basketball. The red defense didn't switch off as they had been taught, and Ricky broke free. He was three yards clear of Ronny, who was the closest red player to him. Jack threw a perfect strike to Ricky, who caught it and made a layup with one second left. Ronny pushed him from behind and was called for a foul. Ricky made the free throw for a three-point lead. Jack again called time-out. There was no such thing as a three-point shot then, so Jack coached everyone to just stand near mid-court and let the red team do whatever they wanted. A long pass was caught near the basket, but the last-second shot missed. It wouldn't have mattered—the white had won.

The next Monday, the boys from the white team

were still buzzing about their big win. Jack's JV coach wished him luck since the list of varsity players would be posted later in the day. When it was, Ronny's name was there, but Jack's name was not. It was a bitter disappointment and would end up leading to a rift between Jack and his dad. Jack was offered the chance to play on the JV team again under the same coach. He would be the only junior on the team. It was an honor that the coaches recognized he deserved to play on a WCHS team because of his dedication and hustle. But in the end, Jack decided he didn't want to suffer the embarrassment of being on the JV team as a junior, playing with freshman and sophomores. Over Matt's strong objection, Jack declined the offer and gave up on his dream of playing varsity basketball

Matt was highly disappointed about Jack's decision. Matt blamed Ricky and some of Jack's other friends for convincing him he shouldn't play on the JV team. Matt had always played sports in high school, even after he got married. He credited his involvement with getting him to graduation. He didn't want to see Jack give up on basketball so easily. Matt had never truly recognized how academically gifted Jack was and instead saw sports as something Jack needed to do to stay engaged in school.

14

MATT THE FAMILY MAN

Jack's parents had married at a very young age, when Matt was sixteen and Mary was fourteen. Just before Mary's sixteenth birthday, Carol was born. Surprisingly, they both managed to finish high school. Matt always said it was sports that kept him in school. He played basketball and baseball and also ran track. His graduating class had only thirty-three members, so he had little competition and excelled in all three sports. He was also more athletic than Jack. Matt tied for first in the region in the mile run in his senior year. He had never run the mile, but the boy who usually did was sick that day. The coach asked Matt to sub. He ran his heart out and caught the leader and race favorite at the finishing tape—a dead heat.

Because sports had played such an important role in his life, Matt didn't understand Jack's decision to quit basketball. They argued about it a few times, with Matt mostly blaming Ricky and Jack's other friends for influencing him. Jack admitted that his friends thought he would be crazy to play, but he insisted the decision was his own. He didn't believe he could ever achieve his dream and didn't want to continue chasing it. Matt reluctantly accepted Jack's decision and never mentioned it again. Unfortunately, things were never quite the same between them after that. Matt felt Jack had tossed away the part of himself he had inherited from his father. Jack had always felt Matt didn't really understand what a good student he was and never considered Jack's academic accomplishments to be as important as sports.

Matt had always believed family vacations were important. Every paycheck, he put a little money aside for summer vacation. Every year, he rented a pop-up camper, and they drove to the mountains, usually in North Carolina. The family would do something together each day—visit the Native American town of Cherokee, drive the scenic Great Smoky Mountains National Park highway, play putt-putt golf, or fish for rainbow trout. Fish would always be on the supper menu. The family cooked breakfast and dinner in camp and packed lunch for a picnic. Jack, Tom, and Carol had always enjoyed these trips, especially the time together.

On one occasion, Matt took the family to an Atlanta Braves game. They sat in the stands in left field, right behind the Braves slugger Hank Aaron.

Jack was only ten at the time, and this was a big thrill for him. It was better than being at Yankee Stadium when he was six and seeing Mickey Mantle play. The Braves won that night, and Aaron hit a home run. Jack talked about it for months and kept the program his dad had bought for him.

As the years passed, Carol and Tom followed in their parents' footsteps with their own families. They ate supper together, went on inexpensive but fun vacations, attended church together, and emphasized the importance of family unity. Their children played various sports, and the parents always attended their games. So did Matt and Mary. Matt was, of course, their coach in basketball, and the wins kept coming. Matt kept a collection of trophies in the room Jack and Tom had shared growing up.

Jack had always enjoyed the family vacations when he was younger, but that had changed as he started high school. Ricky had played a part in Jack's change of attitude, though not intentionally. Ricky and his family had moved to Woodberry at the beginning of freshman year, and he and Jack had quickly become best friends. Both of Ricky's parents owned businesses and had moved the headquarters of both. It was obvious they had plenty of money. Their vacations didn't involve pop-up campers or rainbow trout fried on a pan over an open fire. They stayed in nice hotels in New York City, San Francisco, and even Hawaii.

When they went to Braves games, as they frequently did, their seats were close enough to the field to feel the sweat flying off a batter as he ran to first base.

Whenever Ricky told Jack about these vacations, he wasn't bragging, but Jack took it that way. He didn't tell Ricky about his family's vacations. He was jealous and wished his family had the money to do those things. What Jack never noticed was that Ricky's parents were never at his games, never picked him up from practice, and were rarely home at the end of the day when Ricky's day was over. Ricky's parents worked long hours, and Ricky didn't see them nearly as much as Jack saw his parents. All Jack saw was all the things Ricky got to do, and he wanted those things too.

After their junior year, Ricky invited Jack to join his family at Jekyll Island, on the coast of Georgia. For a week, they stayed in a luxurious beachside condominium. Jack and Ricky spent time on the beach, played putt-putt and regular golf, and rode bikes. They ate every meal out. At night, the entire family would go to dinner together. Ricky's parents paid for everything. Of course, they didn't spend much time with the teens during the day. They were busy working. Jack didn't notice that. He had never told Ricky much about his own family vacations. After that week, he never would.

During high school, Jack was seemingly embarrassed by everything that showed his friends the state of his family's finances. Upon turning sixteen, many of his friends were provided a car to drive. Not Jack. Of course, he always had a car to use or a ride whenever he needed it, but that didn't matter to him. He was jealous of his friends. Ricky got a brand-new car for his sixteenth birthday. It was nicer than the car Ricky's father drove.

Jack's friends all had brand-name stereos too. For Christmas, Jack got a store-brand stereo from Sears. It sounded good, and Jack enjoyed playing his music on it, but he was embarrassed to tell his friends the brand of his stereo. Even clothes were an issue to Jack. Levi's blue jeans and Adidas tennis shoes were the marks of money in their school. Jack wore plain-pocket jeans from JCPenney and off-brand tennis shoes. What he didn't know was that most high schoolers didn't notice such things nearly as much as he did.

It was during those high school years that Jack grew so cynical about the world and money. It was those years that turned him into the money-hungry man who cared only about growing his wealth and not having his family go without the things that he thought he had missed in his childhood.

> He who loves money will not be satisfied with money, nor he who loves wealth with his income; this is vanity.
> —Ecclesiastes 5:10 (ESV)

You shall not covet your neighbor's house. You shall not covet your neighbor's wife, or his male or female servant, his ox or his donkey, or anything that that belongs to your neighbor.

—Exodus 20:17 (NIV)

A heart at peace gives life to the body, but envy rots the bones.

—Proverbs 14:30 (NIV)

15

MARRIAGE ON THE BRINK

Chloe had come along in November 2000. She was a beautiful baby, and Regina was a wonderful mom. William had started preschool, giving Regina and Chloe plenty of mother–daughter bonding time. Jack continued his same old routine. He had always said that becoming a partner at Brooks would allow him more time away from the office. But that was not true. If anything, he spent more time there. Even if he wasn't at the office, he was constantly working on something work-related—answering emails, writing letters, working on closing arguments, or returning phone calls at all hours. He had become one of the best litigators in the city, but the life of a litigator really belonged to the clients.

Over the next seven years, Jack didn't show he had learned anything from his parents about raising a family. His role was to provide the money and plenty of it. Everything else fell to Regina. She made sure the kids got to school, kept them fed, helped them with homework, took them to activities, and did anything else associated with raising children. Jack went to the office, stayed there late most days, and had minimal contact with his children. Jack often missed their activities and convinced himself that his high level of income justified his absence from their everyday lives.

> Husbands, love your wives well! Your children are noticing how you treat her. You are teaching your sons how they should treat women, and you are teaching your daughters what they should expect from men.

"You told William you would be at his game today," Regina said angrily. "He cried when you didn't show up. Stop making promises you can't or won't keep."

"Good grief, what do you want from me? I can't just blow off clients whenever I want."

Regina shot back, "That's all you seem to care about. Do you want to be a father like the one you had or like mine?"

"At least your father isn't still working when he's seventy."

"Yeah, and now my dad has plenty of time for golf, card games, and hanging out at the club. He spends practically no time with Mom. Your father shows more interest in William and Chloe than my father, and he's three hundred miles away."

"Your mom has always been able to do anything she wanted."

"Except spend much time with her husband. She always wanted him to be more available to us. All he cared about was making money. He thought it was all we needed. Sound familiar?"

> And again I say unto you, it is easier for a camel to go through the eye of a needle, than for a rich man to enter into the kingdom of God.
> —Matthew 19:24

These conversations were frequent. Neither of them would sleep in another room, but instead one of them stayed up half the night, avoiding the bedroom.

After twenty years of marriage and eleven years of being a mother, Regina did something she had never thought she would do. She made an appointment with a domestic relations attorney. Even though she was an attorney too, Regina knew she needed the advice of an expert if she was going to leave Jack. It broke her heart to even schedule the appointment. She still loved Jack, and even though he was an absent father,

Regina felt that a broken home would be even worse for the children.

On the day of her appointment with a divorce lawyer, Regina got a phone call from Mary Hodges. The news put Regina's plans on hold.

16

A TERRIBLE LOSS

In March 2008, at the age of seventy, Matt Hodges suffered a major heart attack and died before an ambulance could reach the house where he had lived for forty-five years. He had also worked at the same job for forty-five years and had retired just one month before. The most recent group of little basketball players had just won another city championship with Matt as coach. He had become known as the Wizard of Woodberry, after coaching legend John Wooden, who won ten NCAA basketball championships at UCLA. Matt had been coaching rec league basketball for over thirty-five years.

When Jack got the news, he made arrangements to be gone from the office on Monday and Tuesday. Matt had died on a Friday, and the tradition was that the funeral would be Sunday afternoon or Monday. Jack figured he could stay until late Tuesday afternoon and then drive home. He made a hotel reservation at the only decent hotel in Woodberry, the Holiday Inn where Jack had worked during high school. He went home to pack and found the house somber. The kids were eleven and seven now. They had never dealt with a family death, but they definitely understood that they would never see their grandpa again. Jack had never made much effort to foster his children's relationship with their grandparents, but Regina had been vigilant about it. Her parents lived in Atlanta, and her mother saw the children frequently. Regina had always wanted the kids to have the opportunity to know the rest of their family. To that end, she drove the kids down to Woodberry as much as possible so that William and Chloe would know their grandparents, aunts, uncles, and cousins.

Regina told Jack his mom had called to tell her their rooms would be ready for them.

"I have a reservation for us at the Holiday Inn."

"We're not staying in a hotel. Your mother needs her family in the house with her, and we will be there."

"We'll just be in the way," Jack replied. "Their church people will take care of her."

"She needs *us*, and we will be there for her. You can stay wherever you want, but the kids and I will be at your mother's house. You're her son, for heaven's sake."

Without another word, Jack called to cancel the room at the Holiday Inn. He packed his clothes and loaded the car, and they left for the drive south.

Mary greeted them at the door with hugs, tears, and a gracious demeanor that spoke volumes about her faith. Mary's father, Paul, had helped start a church in Woodberry in the late 1930s. Mary had gone to church all throughout her childhood and adult life. Her constant attendance was not out of any sense of obligation. She had become a Christian when she was twelve and had been devoted to her faith ever since.

Mary Johnson had developed a crush on Matt when she was a first grader. He was an older, wiser second grader, and the two of them bonded from the beginning. After they finished the eighth and ninth grades, respectively, Mary and Matt got married. That was the summer of 1954. They had spent very few nights apart since. Carol had been born in September 1955, Tom in 1958, and Jack in 1962.

> Train up a child in the way he should go; and when he is old he will not depart from it.
>
> —Proverbs 22:6 (KJV)

17

A SMALL TOWN SAYS GOODBYE TO A BIG MAN

On Sunday afternoon, the family arrived at the funeral home for visitation. Nothing could have prepared Jack for what he would see that day. The visitors were seemingly endless. The line of people waiting to view Matt and pay their respects to the family stretched out the funeral home door, down the sidewalk, and out of sight around a street corner. Three hours passed before the crowd began to thin out. Woodberry was a small town of about thirty-five thousand people. It seemed that all of them had shown up and then some. Like many southern towns, Woodberry was divided largely along racial lines. That division was true even in the schools. The city and county each had their own school system. The city high school was about 65 percent black, while the county high school was only 10 percent black. There was no racial division that day.

Whites and blacks showed up in droves to say goodbye to Matt Hodges.

So many people showed up with their families in tow. Jack didn't know why at first, but by the end of afternoon, he would have a better understanding of what his father meant to so many people in this small town. There were some of Matt's high school classmates, friends from childhood, people Matt had worked with, deacons who had served with him at church, other church members, and then an assortment of other people with various connections to the man. Of course, Matt's family was there in full force. He came from a family of ten kids, and there were still six survivors. All of them were there except one, along with their spouses and some of their children.

Many of the visitors were former basketball players Matt had coached. Some of them had children Matt had coached. Most of them didn't talk about his being a good coach or about how they had won so many games. They told stories of his humanity. More than one man told a story of Matt buying shoes for him so he could play basketball. Others talked about how Matt would give them rides to practices and games because their parents couldn't or wouldn't get them there. Without him, they couldn't have played. Many of them came from poor broken homes. The rec league charged just a few dollars to play in the league, but many of them couldn't afford it. It didn't matter. Matt made sure all of them could play.

Through the course of the afternoon, other visitors told stories about how Matt and Mary had helped them through the years. Mary cooked for people. Matt did odd jobs at their homes, gave rides to people with no transportation, babysat kids so parents could have one night out together, bought medicine for people who couldn't afford it, and delivered canned goods to the doorsteps of people in need. Similar stories were told over and over and over.

One couple related how Matt had headed up a project to replace their roof when it was old and worn out, allowing the hard summer rains to leak into the house. Matt had spent his entire weekend working in the hot sun on that roof while the couple was gone away to visit family. Upon their return on Sunday night, they found a new roof on the house and boxes of canned goods in the garage. For about two years, the couple didn't know who had spearheaded the project. When they finally found out, they went to the Hodges home to say thank you. Matt and Mary denied knowing anything about it. Matt said he had helped, but that was all he knew. In the end, Mary gave them a pie she had just taken out of the oven and sent them on their way. At the visitation, the couple told Jack about his parents' kindness but never said

anything to Mary. It had always been understood that
no thanks was necessary.

A theme emerged from the stories of Matt's
kindness. He and Mary had given of themselves
throughout their lives. They didn't expect thanks.
They weren't seeking awards. They often never knew
the impact they were having on the lives of others. In
fact, they sometimes didn't remember the names of
the people they had helped. To them, it wasn't about
keeping score. It was about faith in God, being kind
to others, and living their lives as Jesus commanded.

> Then the King will say to those on his
> right, "Come, you who are blessed by
> my Father; take your inheritance, the
> kingdom prepared for you since the
> creation of the world. For I was hungry
> and you gave me something to eat, I was
> thirsty and you gave me something to
> drink, I was a stranger and you invited me
> in, I needed clothes and you clothed me,
> I was sick and you looked after me, I was
> in prison and you came to visit me." Then
> the righteous will answer him, "Lord,
> when did we see you hungry and feed
> you, or thirsty and give you something to
> drink? When did we see you a stranger
> and invite you in, or needing clothes and

clothe you? When did we see you sick or
in prison and go to visit you?" The King
will reply, "Truly I tell you, whatever you
did for one of the least of these brothers
and sisters of mine, you did for me."
—Matthew 25:34–40 (NIV)

At the funeral on Monday, there was more of the
same. Five different people spoke just to tell a story
about how Matt had impacted their lives in some
way. All the stories involved acts of kindness and
generosity. A couple of the stories included Matt using
his own money to assist the speaker. Matt was not a
wealthy man, but he gave anyway. The stories had
commonalities—the good deed was done anonymously,
if possible, or at least with no fanfare; no recognition or
reward was expected; the effort required of Matt was
downplayed by him; and each act was remembered by
the recipient long after Matt had forgotten about it.
The church could comfortably seat about 375 people.
For the service, there were extra chairs in aisles, rows
of seats in the vestibule, and chairs down any hallway
that connected to the sanctuary. It was probably a
good thing the fire marshal wasn't friends with Matt.

Jack was somber but didn't shed any tears. Carol
and Tom were devastated by their loss and wore their
emotions for all to see. All seven of the grandchildren
were visibly upset. Matt's brothers and sisters were

there. Matt had become the patriarch of the family, the one they turned to when they needed advice or help, a shoulder to cry on, or just someone to listen. Now he was gone, and they were all there to show their immense respect for him.

Grown men cried. The pastor joined them during his message. There were light moments too. Matt was a well-known joker who had often told stories that suckered the listeners in until he delivered the punch line. Some of those jokes were repeated and drew some laughs. If there could be a highlight to a funeral, it was when Matt's nephew, thirty-year-old Randall, sang "How Great Thou Art." It was Matt's favorite song.

> *"When Christ shall come,*
> *with royal acclimation,*
> *And take me home, what*
> *joy will fill my heart.*
> *Then I will bow, in humble adoration,*
> *And there proclaim, My God*
> *how great thou art."*

When the service was over, the casket was loaded into the hearse for the procession to the cemetery. The lead cars likely arrived at the graveyard before the last cars even left the church. There was a short service at the graveside, and then the family went back to the church for lunch. During lunch, an endless line of people wished the family well, offered to help in any way they could, and continued telling stories about the good deeds of Matt Hodges—the Wizard of Woodberry, deacon of the church, husband, father, grandfather, brother, uncle, friend, Christian. His wife of over fifty-five years was amazingly strong throughout the day. It was obvious she was deeply saddened by her loss. She silently wept during parts of the funeral service. Her face was etched with grief. But she remained composed, a pillar of strength for her family. When lunch was over, she approached the podium. She had never been comfortable speaking in public. She thanked everyone for coming, said Matt would have been pleased, and told everyone she looked forward to the day when she would be reunited with Matt, and they would praise God for eternity.

> People will come from east and west and north and south, and will take their places at the feast in the kingdom of God.
> —Luke 13:29–33 (NIV)

18

SETTLING MATTERS

On Tuesday morning, Regina and the kids left to go home. Regina didn't want them to miss a third straight day of school. William had recently missed a week of school with the flu. Jack stayed in Woodberry after calling the office to tell his secretary he would be gone all week. His mother had asked him to stay, and Regina had pushed him about it. He had his laptop with him and could get some work done remotely.

Jack spent the rest of Tuesday helping his mom clean up after all the guests in the house over the previous four days. They visited the bank, the social security office, and an attorney who was a longtime friend and who frequently handled probate. They contacted Matt's former employer to find out what benefits Mary would receive as the widow of a retiree.

Not surprisingly, Matt had chosen a pension option that paid less but would continue for as long as either of them survived. Mary would lose her own social security but would draw Matt's monthly check, which was much higher than hers. In short, Matt had ensured his wife would be well taken care of.

The attorney informed them that probate would be required to give Mary full ownership of the couple's home. Otherwise, all assets passed directly to Mary. The deed to the home had been written in the 1970s and did not include language establishing the ownership as joint with rights of survivorship. Joint ownership would have meant the home could pass directly to the surviving spouse without a probate. Without the proper language, probate was required. The attorney did say that the probate could be relatively simple, and he would handle everything.

Before he left the attorney's office, Jack asked the attorney to review the deeds for Carol's and Tom's homes. Both of them had been prepared the old, inefficient way too. Jack told the attorney he would talk to Carol and Tom to tell them they should take care of this issue. It would be easy, inexpensive, and worthwhile to correct this problem and avoid the headache of probate.

After they finished their errands, Mary and Jack went home. Jack returned some calls while his mom cooked supper. After they ate, Mary left for her Tuesday night Bible study, and Jack was alone in the house. He watched television for a while but really wasn't paying attention. He couldn't stop thinking about all he had heard about his father at the visitation and funeral.

Jack went to the bedroom he and Tom had shared and began to really look around. Basketball trophies and thank-you plaques were everywhere. Jack counted twenty-two trophies for Christmas tournament and league championships. Not bad for thirty-five years of coaching. Of course, in some years Matt had coached more than one team, but his record was still notable. You didn't become known as the Wizard of Woodberry for no reason.

19

AN INFLUENTIAL MAN

The plaques Matt had received from his teams outnumbered the trophies—twenty-eight in all. In truth, most kids and their parents never recognized the hard work and time a coach gave to a team, even in a youth league. The kids and parents from Matt's teams did, and it showed. With him giving kids rides, buying their shoes, and paying fees for some players, it wasn't hard for parents to notice.

Jack opened several drawers in the dresser. In one, he found notes and letters from kids Matt had coached over the years. Some had been written soon after a season ended. Some had been written years after a kid played for Matt. These were young men and women whose lives had been impacted so much that they had written letters to Matt years later. A letter from one young man stood out among all the others.

Dear Coach Hodges,

You may not remember me but I was on your basketball team in 1988. This letter is long overdue, but I wanted to thank you for all you did for me. When I signed up to play on your team, my mom didn't have the money for me to play or to get me a pair of decent shoes to play in. You paid my fees and bought me a pair of shoes. On those days when my mom was working late, you gave me a ride to practice or games. I loved playing basketball and ended up getting a scholarship to play at University of South Florida. I am a high school teacher and JV basketball coach now. I just pray I can help my players as much as you helped me.

God bless you,
Micah Jones

This letter was just one of many.

Micah Jones had been a basketball star at Woodberry High. He was a terrific point guard and had led Woodberry to the state finals, where they had lost on a buzzer-beater shot from twenty-five feet. He had gone on to South Florida, played basketball for four years, and graduated with an education degree. Matt had always told his players to stay in school and study. After graduation, Micah had gotten married and accepted a teaching and coaching job at a Tampa high school. He had also started a family—two sons. Both were basketball players and had their own father as their coach.

Needless to say, Matt had been a positive influence on many lives, including countless kids and teens. Jack had never realized this, until it was too late to appreciate it.

> People may not remember what you said or what you did, but they will remember how you made them feel.
>
> —Unknown

20

CHILDHOOD MEMORIES SAVED

In two other drawers, Jack found all kinds of papers and other items from his and Tom's time in the house. There was one drawer for Tom and one for Jack. He couldn't believe all the things he found in his drawer—his kindergarten report card, newspaper clippings from games (including the one reporting Jack's only touchdown), team pictures, certificates he'd received in school, his acceptance letter from Duke, a clipping from the local paper of the Duke dean's list, the scorecard from his score of 86 in that high school golf match, an autographed picture of Roger Staubach, the program from that Braves game when Jack was ten, and a letter from President Jimmy Carter congratulating him on his high school graduation. Jack had long since forgotten about all these items. His parents hadn't forgotten and had never thrown them away.

Jack didn't realize how late it had gotten. He had been so engrossed in what he was doing that he didn't hear his mom come in from Bible study. It was about 11:30 p.m. when she knocked on the door and told him she was going to bed. He opened the door to say good night. Instinctively, he hugged her and told her he loved her. He had not said that to her in a long time. He called Regina, asked about the kids, talked a few minutes about nothing at all, and got into bed. Before he fell asleep, Jack cried for the first time since he had been told about his father's death.

For the next few days, Jack did some work on an appellate brief that was due the following week, answered emails, returned phone calls, and spent time with his mom. As little as he had talked to his dad over the last few years, he had talked to her even less. Surprisingly, conversation was easy. Mary had never talked much when Matt was around. He had been such a talker who just naturally carried a conversation. He didn't do it on purpose or out of ego; it was just his personality. With Matt gone, she talked almost constantly. She told Jack about their relatives and friends whose names Jack recognized from his childhood, and she even talked about William and Chloe. Jack found she knew as much about his children's lives as he did—thanks to Regina.

21

THE MAN IN THE MIRROR

Blessed are those who mourn, for they
shall be comforted.
                    —Matthew 5:4 (NIV)

On Saturday, Carol and Tom came over to the house.
Jack had not seen much of them since the funeral.
They both had gone back to work on Wednesday,
probably preferring to keep busy rather than have too
much idle time to think about their loss. Talk between
them and Jack was labored, as it had been for years.
Jack didn't feel they had anything in common. He
did tell them about the things he and their mom had
done earlier in the week. He also explained the issue
about the title to the house and probate and relayed to
them what the attorney had told him about the deeds
to their own homes.

In truth, Jack was glad when it got to be late
afternoon and Carol and Tom went home. Jack called

Ricky and invited him to dinner Saturday night. Ricky had moved away from Woodberry in his early twenties, gotten married, had a son, and then divorced. He now had moved back to Woodberry and married a woman who also had graduated with them. Jack had never known Marie very well, but Ricky seemed happy. Ricky was the only high school classmate Jack had ever kept in touch with.

Woodberry was not very well known for restaurants, or anything else for that matter, so they drove fifty miles to Brunswick, on the coast of Georgia. They ate seafood and talked a little about their current lives but spent most of their time talking about their high school years and the good times they'd had back then. It saddened Jack some that they had nothing in common except their past. After dinner, Ricky dropped Jack at a rental car company. Regina had offered to drive to Woodberry for the weekend to get him home, but Jack had declined. He thought the time alone in the car would give him time to think. He needed that.

The next morning, Jack ate breakfast, had two cups of coffee, packed the car, said his goodbyes to his Mom, Carol, and Tom, and headed for home. The drive was about 275 miles, much of it two-lane roads. That five hours in the car would become for Jack a journey of soul-searching and discovery.

The drive itself was uneventful and gave Jack a great opportunity for reflection about his past, present, and future. Early in the trip, he replayed in his mind all he had seen, heard, and learned about his father, his mother, and the immense respect they had earned over the years from all the people whose lives they'd touched. He thought a lot about all his parents had done for him, Carol, and Tom. Baseball games, piano lessons, basketball practices and games, plays, chorale concerts, weekly golf matches, academic awards ceremonies, church activities—you name it, they were always there. If only one child had an activity, then both parents would attend. If their children's activities conflicted, they would divide and conquer to make sure all the kids felt supported.

Then Jack thought about all the people he had met at the visitation and funeral and the stories they'd told about all the ways Matt had helped them, taught them, and encouraged them. Matt had treated everyone with kindness. He'd had a long-lasting impact on so many lives. It occurred to Jack that in contrast, anything he himself had done for anyone over the last twenty years had been for selfish reasons. His good deeds had nothing to do with kindness, faith, or Christianity. What he expected to get out of his supposed good deeds was always the same—to receive recognition, curry favor to further his career, or be seen by the right people. My God, he thought, was he really that shallow?

Jack didn't shed any tears, but he was quite somber.

It was a terrible feeling when the reflection you saw in a mirror was a person you neither liked nor ever really wanted to be. Jack now realized how self-absorbed he had become. He stopped at Chick-Fil-A for lunch. The restaurant was packed, but he wanted a break from driving. The only open table was near the indoor playground. As he ate, Jack watched the kids playing, and his thoughts turned to his own children. He had missed so much of their lives because he had allowed his career and greed to control his own life.

He got back on the road, with a stream of guilt dominating his thoughts. One after another, he remembered events in his children's lives and in Regina's life that he had missed because he was too busy chasing his partnership obsession, hobnobbing with the well-to-do, and worshiping the almighty dollar.

About five years after law school, Regina had been recognized at a banquet for her legal and charitable work with low-income families. Jack had known about the event for a month. At the last minute, a Brooks & Duncan partner, Paul Wilson, called Jack into his office to discuss a case. The meeting could have waited, but Jack was too concerned about his image to tell the partner he needed to leave. He stayed in Wilson's office too long to make the banquet. That night, Jack knew Regina was terribly hurt by his absence at the banquet, but neither spoke about it, or about anything else for that matter.

The next morning, Paul Wilson knocked on Jack's door. "Got a minute?" Paul asked.

Jack was surprised to see a partner at his door but invited Paul in.

"I understand you missed an event yesterday to talk with me about the McCutcheon case."

"How did you know that?" Jack asked.

"Your secretary saw mine in the break room this morning and told her about it. Jack, let me give some free advice. When I was new here, I was much like you. I worked long hours and was interested only in a partnership. My wife got sick of my lack of attention to her and the kids. She left and took the children with her."

"I'm sorry. I didn't know you were divorced," replied Jack.

"If you think this firm and your clients are worth being alone, you need to think again. I have always regretted my failures as a husband and father." Paul continued, "I have managed to somewhat mend my relationships with my daughters, and I have become a part of their children's lives, but there is always something missing. My girls may have forgiven me for my absence from their childhood, but they are still somewhat guarded with me. I wish I had made different decisions back then."

"I think when I become partner, I can be a better husband. We don't have any kids yet," said Jack.

Paul smirked and then said, "Changing your work habits is easier said than done. All you care about is work, and everyone here knows it. That may boost your chances in the minds of some partners, but your reputation as a human being suffers in the meantime. Don't ruin your relationship with your wife over this place. It isn't worth it."

Unfortunately, Jack didn't heed that sage advice.

When William was a second grader, his class was doing a short play just after lunch. William had the lead role. When it was time to start, all the kids were peeking from behind the curtain to catch a glimpse of their parents and grandparents. William smiled when he saw his mom, who waved and gave him a big grin. William's smile disappeared, though, as he searched all over the auditorium for his dad. Jack was not there. He had allowed a phone conference to start later than scheduled, and it went through lunch.

Chloe took dance lessons when she was six. One afternoon, parents were invited to watch a short performance after class, beginning around 4:45 p.m. Regina couldn't be there and stressed to Jack how much it would disappoint Chloe if he was not there to see her dance. He promised. When the performance was over, many of the girls received flowers from a parent in attendance. Chloe had only her babysitter for the day—a college student she barely knew. Jack finally made it just as refreshment time was ending. The disappointment was evident on Chloe's face. She never cried, but the usual chatterbox didn't speak a word during the ride home.

At nine, William started playing little league baseball. His grandpa Matt had told him all about how much fun Jack had had playing as a kid. In his fourth game of the season, William hit a hard shot between the center and right fielders. The ball rolled all the way to the fence. Before the outfielders could reach the ball and throw it to the infield, William was rounding third. He easily beat the throw to the plate for an inside-the-park home run. Jack only got to hear about it later from Regina. He wasn't there to see it.

There were too many similar stories to remember them all, but several more flashed into Jack's head. With few exceptions, he had allowed work to take precedence over his family. He had never felt so ashamed in his life.

During that drive, Jack also thought about his career. He thought about the clients he represented, the cases he had been involved in, and most significantly, the issues he had dealt with as a lawyer doing mostly insurance defense and corporate litigation. He asked himself a question: how many people whom he had represented would show up at his funeral, let alone tell any stories about how he had helped them? He couldn't think of a single one. All the work he had ever done was about making money, holding on to money, or not paying money to an injured person who really needed and deserved it. The only thing that might be true was that some of the plaintiffs with cases against his clients might show up to pray for his soul.

When Jack was about forty miles from home, he pulled into a rest area and parked where no one could see him. He had never felt so alone, ashamed, or empty. Overcome by emotion, he buried his face in his hands and cried uncontrollably. He didn't stop for a long time. When he had gained some control over himself, Jack did something he had not sincerely done in a long time—he prayed. In that private moment with God, Jack realized that the events of the past week had been leading him to one inescapable truth—he needed to make some changes in his life.

22

A NEW JACK

Over the next week, Jack worked shorter hours and was home in time for dinner every night. The family was glad to have him there, but he was in a subdued mood and didn't talk much. On Sunday morning, Regina got dressed for church, got the kids up, and cooked breakfast. Regina, William, and Chloe were sitting at the table in their Sunday clothes when Jack walked in without a word. He was wearing a suit. He poured a cup of coffee and sat down.

Chloe said, "Daddy, my choir is singing at church this morning."

"I can't wait to hear it."

Jack attended church with the family that morning for the first time in years, except his annual Easter Sunday appearance.

Over the next few weeks, Jack spent more time with the family and showed a real interest in the children's daily lives. Regina was cautious but decided to hold off on the appointment with the divorce lawyer. Jack also had been more attentive to her right after he made partner at Brooks and Duncan, but it hadn't lasted. Regina wanted to see if Jack was really changing or if he was just reacting to his father's death and to hearing about what Matt Hodges had meant to the people around him. Maybe his behavior was just being driven by guilt and not a real change of heart.

For the next few months, Jack continued to come home from work earlier than in the past, went to church with the family, and attended many of the children's activities. His relationship with Regina improved also. They had friends over a few times and went on a few dates for dinner, a movie, and even dancing. On the Fourth of July, they had a yard full of friends and their families over. Jack even manned the grill. He still worked long hours, going in early and bringing work home to do after the kids were in bed, but family time did seem to be more of a priority to him.

Regardless of whether the change was permanent, Jack took two days off and an entire weekend to watch Chloe swim at the state swimming championships in late July. He had occasionally gone to meets but had never made being there a priority. On this weekend, Jack went to the meet, volunteered to be a timer at one of the swim sessions, and went to lunch with the family afterwards. When Chloe made the evening finals set for Friday, Jack spent the afternoon at home and drove her back to the pool at Georgia Tech for the evening swim session. He never called the office or checked his email. It was certainly out of character.

Two weekends later, Jack came downstairs on a Saturday dressed as if he was going to the office. Instead, he told the family he had a surprise for them, and they went out for breakfast. Regina beamed as the kids chattered all the way through their meal.

Regina looked at Jack and said, "This was a nice surprise."

Jack replied, "I'm glad you're enjoying breakfast, but this isn't really the surprise."

"What are you up to?"

"You'll see after breakfast," Jack said.

After the family finished breakfast, Jack drove them to an office park off of Peachtree Street, near downtown Atlanta. The park was well-groomed and clean, but not particularly nice. There were about ten individual offices, and each office door was painted neatly with a business name. The park had an eclectic group of businesses, from professional offices to a lawn landscaping company. Jack pulled into a parking space in front of a door covered in brown paper, like a UPS package. The paper also had a big red bow on it. Jack positioned the kids a few feet from the door and told Regina to open her gift. She removed the bow and ripped through the paper. The name of a newly created business was painted on the door: "Hodges & Hodges, Attorneys at Law."

Regina was stunned and speechless. The kids were asking what this meant.

Jack asked Regina, "What do you think, partner?"

Regina still didn't say anything. Jack wasn't sure how she was going to react, so he just kept talking to explain what he had done.

"Brooks & Duncan isn't the right place for me anymore. I quit yesterday. It's time for me to do something that really makes a difference in my clients' lives—and in our lives. That was never going to happen at Brooks. I know I should have discussed this with you, but this change had to be all mine. I don't expect you to really understand that." He continued, "I don't really expect you to come here to work every day either, or any day if you don't want to. But you will have an office anytime you want."

Regina jumped into Jack's arms. "It's OK. It's really OK. I love you."

23

NOT JUST A SOUVENIR

They went inside to look around the new law firm's offices. At the front there was a reception desk and waiting area. A short hallway then led to a small conference room and two offices. They walked into Regina's office first. There was a plaque on the desk, facing two chairs for clients: "Regina Hodges— Attorney at Law." Jack's office was similar. Each office had some paintings on the walls and family pictures on the desk and credenza. The only real difference was that one of Jack's walls was adorned with the hockey stick, hung so that the shaft went up diagonally from the blade, which was level with the floor. The blade of a hockey stick is curved. In the past, the stick had been positioned on Jack's wall so that the blade curved away from the wall. Now the stick was reversed so that the back of the blade could be seen. On it was scrawled "Matthew 16:26."

Jack had seen that verse on the stick many times over the years, but he had never read it.

John Gibson was one of the workers who had moved Jack's office furnishings from Brooks & Duncan to the newly formed firm Hodges & Hodges. He had worked diligently and quietly moving Jack's office furniture, books, and other items into the new office. He had introduced himself to Jack, but there had been little conversation except to ask where things went. That changed when John saw the hockey stick. John asked Jack about the stick, assuming Jack had once used it as a hockey player in his earlier years. Jack told John about the trip to Lake Placid and watching the US team beat the Soviets. John was more interested in the story of the Bible verse but quickly realized Jack didn't know the story behind the verse's presence on the stick. John had his own story. That verse, Matthew 16:26, had a very special meaning to him, he said.

"I was part of corporate America in my earlier days. I was in sales, and I was good at it. I made a lot of money over the years, but there was a price to pay. I was rarely home. When I was home, I worked long hours and missed much of my sons' childhoods. My two sons played football, basketball, and baseball, but I didn't make it to many of their games, or to anything else they did. In the blink of an eye, they went off to college, and the time I'd lost with them was gone forever."

"Sounds familiar. So how did you end up moving furniture?"

"Both of my sons got business degrees and decided to start a moving and storage business together. They started asking me for advice. I appreciated that they would even ask since our relationship had never been that great. So I decided to offer them a deal: all the free advice they wanted in exchange for a small piece of the business and a job."

"So you're in business with your sons," stated Jack.

"Yes, and I couldn't be happier. I don't make nearly as much money as I did in sales, but I get to see my sons practically every day, and my relationship with them has never been better. On top of that, I go home to my wife every night for dinner."

"So what's the deal with the Bible verse on the stick?"

"I came across that verse one night when I was reading the Bible in some hotel room on the road. It was as if the verse had been written specifically for me. Look it up. I think it will mean something to you too."

John obviously knew how the verse would be relevant to Jack. He was familiar with Brooks & Duncan, with its big law-firm trappings. That day, after the movers left, Jack found a Bible and read the verse for the first time. At that moment, Jack knew his move away from Brooks & Duncan was the right one to make. From that moment on, the meaning of the hockey stick was forever changed. Every time he looked at the stick now, he was reminded of how he had seemingly gained the whole world but lost his soul in the process.

Jack didn't know which hockey player had owned the stick or what the verse had meant to that player. But forevermore, the hockey stick would always remind him of what was most important in this world—being a good father, a good husband, a good son, and a good friend.

> For what is a man profited, if he shall gain the whole world, and lose his soul? Or what shall a man give in exchange for his soul?
> —Matthew 16:26 (KJV)

> I will give you a new heart and put a new spirit in you; I will remove from you your heart of stone and give you a heart of flesh.
> —Ezekiel 36:26 (NIV)

Regina smiled the rest of the day. She had prayed for the day Jack would realize how much he had missed, how much the kids needed him, and how much more he had to offer the family than just earning money. Her prayers had been answered. It had taken the death of Jack's father to wake him up to the reality of his life. God didn't always answer prayers the way people wanted Him to answer, but He did answer. Jack had lost his father, the kids a beloved grandfather, and Regina a respected man who had been like a father. Jack, though, had gained perspective.

The family would continue to see changes in Jack.

24

LIKE FATHER, LIKE SON

Over the next few months, Jack continued to attend church, joined a Sunday school class, and went through a new members class so he could become a church member. When the new school year began, Jack signed up for a class called Disciples I. The small group met each Sunday afternoon to discuss an assigned Bible reading, discuss how the scriptures related to their daily lives, and pray. The purpose of the class was an overview of the Bible and to gain a better basic understanding of the scriptures. It was also an opportunity to build Christian relationships with a small group.

Regina and Jack also decided to sell their home during this time. In the past, Jack had believed it was important to live in the "right" place and make a real impression on friends and colleagues. So they had lived in an upscale home in a gated community. Perhaps women more frequently cared about having a "show" home, but in this case Jack had been the one most concerned about the impression his house would create. That didn't matter to him now. They put the house on the market, quickly received an acceptable offer, and then found an older home in the Virginia Highlands area of Atlanta. The home needed some repairs and updating, but they moved in and settled into a new lifestyle. Regina loved the home and the fact that Jack no longer seemed so concerned about what people thought of their house, cars, or clothes. Jack even sold his Mercedes-Benz and bought a Honda Accord.

What the family loved most about this new Jack was his dedication to their lives and their church and his newly found giving spirit. With rare exceptions, he had breakfast with the family before William and Chloe went to school. They ate dinner together most evenings. Jack showed up at school events, sporting events, piano recitals, and almost everything else the family did. He became the "team dad" of William's basketball team and an assistant little league baseball coach. William and Chloe got to know their father better than they ever had before. He helped with homework when needed and basically spent more time just talking to them, asking about their day, getting to know their friends, and fostering their dreams.

Jack also decided that an annual family vacation was a must. They went to New York City, Maine, the

Grand Canyon, Zion National Park, and Alaska and even overseas to Switzerland and Italy. One summer they spent two weeks touring Glacier National Park, Yellowstone, the Grand Tetons, Devil's Tower, Mount Rushmore, and the Badlands. They were creating memories that none of them would ever forget. In the past, Jack had always been stressed and never seemed relaxed during any family trip. Of course, those trips had been few and far between, but no one had minded because the old Jack had sucked the fun out of any vacation anyway. Not the new Jack. On vacation, he was relaxed, fun, and willing to do anything. They rode mules to the bottom of the Grand Canyon, rafted down the Snake River, hiked to the top of Angels Landing in Zion, and flew on a small plane within three miles of the summit of Denali in Alaska. During their trip to Europe, they zip-lined over snow and toured ice caves at the top of Jungfrau in Switzerland and later swam in the Mediterranean Sea.

In church, Jack always attended with the family, who sat together in worship services. They also attended Sunday school. At first, Jack spent the Sunday school hour just listening, not feeling like he had much to add. He was somewhat intimidated by other members of the class, who seemed to know so much about the Bible and faith. Over time, he became more comfortable and would speak up in class from time to time. Finally, one Sunday morning, he surprised everyone when he started talking and didn't stop for quite some time. The class had been discussing the importance of family. Someone said something about how much they had learned by watching their parents. Jack had always been guarded in talking about his past, but that morning, he let his guard down, and his life story came pouring out. The class was mesmerized as he recounted the week he'd spent in Woodberry for his father's funeral and then the drive home that incredible Sunday. It was the first time Jack had ever really allowed anyone other than Regina to see inside him.

25

RAISING THE CHILDREN

As the years passed, Jack and Regina found more time to spend with each other and with the kids. Their marriage was the best it had ever been. The family dedicated themselves to helping others as much as possible. They participated every year in a churchwide event to work on houses belonging to the elderly and low-income families. The mission was to make major repairs the homeowners couldn't afford. They fixed roofs, replaced leaking toilets, cleaned dirty carpets, built accessibility ramps, and did all other kinds of work.

One year, William went away to a youth conference in Indiana. While there, the group packaged meals for overseas shipment. A group returned from the conference with the big idea to raise $75,000 and package a tractor-trailer load of meals. Many adults didn't think they could raise the money and thought the excitement would wear off when the hard work started. They were wrong. On a sunny April day, over 1,200 volunteers from all over Atlanta showed up and packaged 285,000 meals of rice, soy, and nutrients. The meals didn't seem appetizing to the people packaging them, but they would mean the difference between life and death for the people receiving them. The youth would never meet the children they were helping save, but their faith was steadfast that God had led them to do what they did.

Regina and the kids each had their own causes they believed in and worked for. Jack preferred to support their efforts and stay quietly in the background. That was in stark contrast to his old self, who always made sure everyone knew about anything he did for anyone, though that didn't happen very often. Regina, William, and Chloe didn't do their charity work for recognition or awards, but they received some of both. William won a statewide church award for his work in feeding the hungry. Chloe was named "Volunteer of the Year" by a local literacy organization after she convinced a group of about twenty-five students from her school to read weekly to young children and help them learn to read. Regina continued her work with low-income families and the homeless. She was frequently recognized for her work. She humbly accepted the accolades only because of the publicity it gave to her causes. Jack proudly and joyfully watched their efforts, knowing his family was following Jesus' command to "feed my sheep."

> But when you give to the needy, do not let your left hand know what your right hand is doing, so that your giving may be in secret. Then your Father, who sees what is done in secret, will reward you.
> —Matthew 6:3–4 (NIV)

26

JACK'S MISSION

The kids grew up fast. William became valedictorian of his high school class and followed his own path to Vanderbilt University to major in engineering. He made good grades in school and seemed well on his way to a successful career. Of course, William's definition of success wasn't the same as Jack's when he'd left law school. William wanted to find a cure for childhood cancer.

As William started his sophomore year at Vanderbilt, Chloe became a high school freshman and made the swim team at school. She was a year-round swimmer, and such swimmers were crucial to a high school team's success. In her freshman season, she barely missed the all-region team, made state cuts in two events, and contributed to her team's Class AAAA state championship. Chloe was a gregarious teen who was a magnet for new friends. She settled right into high school life.

As soon as Chloe's freshman year was over, Jack left with a group of the church's high school seniors for a mission trip to Guatemala. It was Regina who had suggested he take the trip. Over the years, Jack had supported his family's efforts on various mission projects. It made him happy and proud to support them, but Regina sensed that Jack was still missing something from his life. Now it was his turn to be part of something that belonged to only him. Regina hoped and prayed that Jack could find what he was lacking. She felt she knew, but Jack had to discover it on his own.

The mission team traveled to a poor region of Guatemala about three hours from Guatemala City. They arrived on Saturday and traveled on Sunday to a small town called Chichicastenango, well known for its market. Many Guatemalans relied on the money they made in the market to feed their families. The missionaries had been advised that some bargaining was expected but not to take advantage. Some of the merchants probably didn't think much of Jack's bargaining skills or lack thereof. He bought purses and scarves for Regina and Chloe, a wallet for William, and blankets for all. He paid whatever price the merchant asked, even though part of the game was to bargain for a lower price. With the dollar exchange rate, the goods were still much less expensive than in the United States, and he would have felt guilty paying less than the asking price.

On Monday morning, the mission work actually started. To start the day, Jack was asked to give the morning devotional. He read from the book of Matthew a passage he had heard for the first time at his father's funeral.

> Then the King will say to those on his right, "Come, you who are blessed by my Father; take your inheritance, the kingdom prepared for you since the creation of the world. For I was hungry and you gave me something to eat, I was thirsty and you gave me something to drink, I was a stranger and you invited me in, I needed clothes and you clothed me, I was sick and you looked after me, I was in prison and you came to visit me." Then the righteous will answer him, "Lord, when did we see you hungry and feed you, or thirsty and give you something to drink? When did we see you a stranger and invite you in, or needing clothes and clothe you? When did we see you sick or in prison and go to visit you?" The King will reply, "Truly I tell you, whatever you

did for one of the least of these brothers
and sisters of mine, you did for me."
—Matthew 25:34–40 (NIV)

What followed was an inspirational week of hard
work building a water tower and handwashing basin
for a school, playing with the schoolchildren, and
becoming friends with the adult Guatemalan workers.
The local kids found humor in the Americans'
poor soccer skills. What Jack enjoyed the most
was his developing relationships with the workers,
which seemed better than he would have expected
considering the lack of communication. The group
did have a translator, but he wasn't always nearby. The
workers were employed by the mission that sponsored
the work being done, and they helped make sure the
work was done correctly. They probably found the
Americans' lack of skills with tools humorous, but
they never allowed that to be seen. By the end of the
week, these men had earned Jack's respect for their
skills and dedication. They worked and laughed all
week and got the job done. On Friday afternoon, the
schoolkids performed a beautiful ceremony to dedicate
their new facility and to thank the missionaries for
their work. People in the US would have taken the
work for granted. The project created running water
and a working sink so the kids could wash their hands
with fresh water after using a toilet. To Americans,

such facilities were just expected. In Guatemala, they were celebrated.

The week affirmed to Jack that joy didn't come from wealth or any worldly possession. The Guatemalan people lived in small, crowded houses, many with dirt floors and most without running water. The kids got plenty of food, but true nutrition was lacking. They rarely ate protein. Consequently, the kids were smaller than their peers in the US. Yet these kids were always smiling, laughing, playing, singing, and dancing. In short, they were full of joy.

When the work was done and the ceremony was over, Jack and the other adults gathered the Guatemalan workers to say their thanks and goodbyes. They gave each worker a small gift. Jack gave Victor a brimmed hat to replace the one he wore, which was practically falling apart. Victor gave a big smile and hug and put the hat on his head. Everyone shook hands, and some hugged as they prepared to part ways, probably to never see each other again. Jack closed with a few words that the translator had helped him write. His Spanish was poor, but the workers appreciated the effort and understood his message.

"Hemos tenido el honor de trabajar con ustedes. Gracias por su ensenanza y paciencia. El trabajo que ustedes hacen es importante. Su trabajo cambia vidas en Guatemala. Y Tambien cambio nuestras

Vida en estados Unidos Dios los bendiga y los

cuide asta que nes encontremos otra vez." In English, his words meant "We have been honored to work with you. Thank you for your guidance and patience. The work you do is important. Your work changes lives in Guatemala. It also changes lives in the United States. God bless you and keep you until we meet again."

> Do all the good you can
> By all the means you can
> In all the ways you can
> In all the places you can
> At all the times you can
> To all the people you can
> As long as ever you can
>
> —John Wesley

27

THE JOY WITHIN

On the flight home, Jack started thinking about the past week. He'd had fun playing with the kids, working on the project, and seeing firsthand a people who were joyous despite having very little. He began to feel empty. He reflected on the last few years since he had lost his father. He had made significant changes in his life and in his relationships, and everyone around him seemed happier. But he still felt somewhat empty. What was it going to take for him to get rid of this feeling in the pit of his stomach, this feeling that he would never be truly happy? Maybe he could never overcome the selfishness and greed of his past. He had done everything he felt he could do, but for some reason it wasn't enough.

The next day, Jack attended worship services as the Guatemalan mission team was recognized. The team seemed so happy about their work and what they had accomplished. Many of them seemed to have the same type of glow that Jack had seen in the people of Guatemala. The Guatemalan people seemed quite happy and joyous, even though most of them had nothing compared to even the poorest in the United States. He still felt something was missing for him. After church, Jack asked Pastor Mike Edwards if he could speak to him privately. Jack then told Regina and the kids to go on without him to the lunch they had planned with another family.

When Jack and Pastor Mike were alone, Jack retold the story he had told his Sunday school class so many years ago. He told Pastor Mike about all the things he had done to change his life, to be a better husband and father, and to help other people. During their two hours together, Jack's emotions were a mix of highs and lows. At times, he was ashamed. In the next moment, he would feel happy, especially when talking about his new relationship with his family. When he was done, Jack was emotionally spent. He told Pastor Mike he felt wonderful about all the improvements he had made in his life, but he still felt there was a void that nothing had filled.

When Jack had finished, Pastor Mike stood up and moved to the chair nearest Jack. He placed his hand on Jack's shoulder. It would have been easy for Pastor Mike to get bogged down in Jack's story. He had heard similar stories many times in the past and had learned how to handle these situations. He asked one question. "Have you accepted Jesus Christ as your Lord and Savior?"

That question hit Jack like a ton of bricks. When he was about ten, he had gone to the front of his Baptist church during the invitation time at the end of worship. His grandfather had helped start the church in the 1930s, and everyone in the church knew Jack and his family. Jack told the preacher he wanted to be a Christian. They prayed, and Jack went back to his seat, not feeling any different than he had before. After church was over, many people in the congregation, who had known him his entire life, hugged him, shook his hand, patted him on the back, and congratulated his parents. But to Jack, everything felt the same.

An eternity seemed to pass between Pastor Mike's question and Jack's answer, but the longtime preacher just waited patiently. He seemed to understand that Jack was experiencing a moment of self-reflection.

Finally, Jack realized for the first time what the answer was. "No," he said.

"Do you want to accept Him?"

"Yes."

Jack's next words would never be heard in a sermon. They weren't eloquently spoken like the closing arguments for which Jack had become legendary in the

Atlanta legal community. But unlike those arguments to juries, these words were sincere.

"God, I need you. I have always needed you. I know that now. Please forgive me for my sins, for the person I have been. I know I don't deserve it, but I want Jesus in my life, and I want to give my life fully to Him."

> Everyone who calls on the name of the Lord will be saved.
> —Romans 10:13 (NIV)

> My lips shall greatly rejoice when I sing unto thee; and my soul, which thou hast redeemed.
> —Psalm 71:23 (KJV)

When Jack left Pastor Mike's office, he felt as though he were floating on a cloud. No one was there to congratulate him, hug him, pat him on the back, shake his hand, or praise him. But this time, he felt something inside. If he hadn't known better, Jack might have thought he was about to have a heart attack. He had never experienced this feeling in his chest before, but he knew what it was—pure joy. For the first time in his life, he understood the difference between happiness and joy. He was now truly a Christian.

Happiness is externally triggered and based on other people, things, places, thoughts and events. Joy comes when you make peace with who you are, why you are, and where you are.

—Unknown

28

ANOTHER LOSS

The following Saturday, Jack got up early to take Chloe to swim practice. The pool was on a small side road, near a busy four-lane city street. Jack dropped Chloe off and was planning to hit his favorite coffee shop to drink coffee and read the paper while Chloe was swimming. He approached the red light and waited to turn left. The light turned green, and he started into the intersection.

Bill Mayer was not familiar with Georgia Highway 246 and was approaching its intersection with the small road just as Jack was turning left. Bill was in the left lane, and a truck was to his right, slowing down to stop at the red light. The sun was imperfectly positioned and made it hard to see that there was even a traffic light in the intersection. Bill never saw it. He barreled through the intersection at fifty miles per hour and plowed into Jack's Honda

Accord, hitting the left front corner of the vehicle as it turned left.

When the vehicles came to rest, Jack sat unconscious in the driver's seat of his car. Airbags from the steering wheel and driver's side door had activated and probably prevented any serious harm from the neck down. After first responders freed him from the vehicle, an ambulance rushed Jack to the nearest emergency room at one of Atlanta's largest hospitals. He was still unconscious, and the extent of his injuries was unknown.

Regina was on a women's retreat in North Carolina that weekend. Two of her close friends drove her back to Atlanta. Regina was on the phone most of the trip. Swim team parents had learned of the accident before practice was over and had taken Chloe home with them and their children. Regina's parents would pick Chloe up and go to the Hodges home to wait. Regina didn't want Chloe at the hospital unless her mother was there. Regina next called William, who was in Nashville for a summer internship, and then called Mary, Carol, and Tom.

Regina also talked with doctors at the hospital during the drive, but they didn't know much at that point. They were performing a battery of tests. Jack seemed to have suffered some type of neurological injury, but they didn't know the extent of the damage. When Regina talked to William, he wanted to pack a bag and head for home, but she persuaded him to wait for more concrete information on his dad's condition.

Regina arrived at the hospital and stayed there all night. Jack was in a coma. From the neck down, Jack's injuries were relatively minor. He did have some cracked and broken ribs, but no severe injuries. His major organs were not damaged. He had suffered swelling of the brain, which had been relieved through a surgical procedure. The doctor advised that they should try to keep him stable and then perform additional tests on Monday to determine the extent of injury and the amount of brain activity. On Sunday night, William drove home from Nashville.

First thing Monday morning, Jack underwent a CT scan of his brain. The news was not good. The accident had caused a severe whiplash-like injury, much like the one that had killed NASCAR driver Dale Earnhardt, but Jack's injury was not quite as severe. Earnhardt had died soon after his two-hundred-mile-per-hour accident. Jack had survived two days since the accident, but he showed few signs of brain activity.

Regina called Jack's mom to break the news. After first hearing about the accident, she had stayed in Woodberry, waiting until more was known about Jack's condition. Carol and Tom made the necessary arrangements to be gone and drove their mother to

Atlanta, arriving around dinnertime. Jack's doctors decided to keep him stable for two more days and then perform the same tests they had done immediately after the accident.

On Tuesday, the family spent most of the day at the Hodges house. That was more comfortable than sitting at the hospital. All day, the family talked, prepared and ate meals together, entertained a few visitors, and prayed for healing. Again, Mary was a pillar of strength. She told William and Chloe how proud she was of them and their parents. She spoke of the joy she had felt watching Jack change his life. It was like seeing the prodigal son come back home. Carol and Tom told Regina about some of the things Jack had done for them and their mom over the past few years, almost all of which had been gifts of money to help them out. Regina had never known. She did know Jack never would have done anything for them before their dad died. Their stories made Regina smile.

On Wednesday, Regina was up early. She was anxious. Although her brain told her that her husband's condition likely had not changed, her heart wanted to believe a miracle would occur. By midmorning, the entire family had arrived at the hospital and gathered in a waiting room nearest the intensive care unit. Pastor Mike and a few other church friends joined them. After what seemed like an eternity, they saw

Jack's doctor walking down the hall toward them. Their collective hearts skipped a beat.

The news was not good. Jack's condition had not changed. The level of brain activity was nearly zero. The man they knew and loved was no longer with them. He had been gone the second his car was struck in that intersection.

29

A PAINFUL DECISION

After the family had had some time alone to comfort each other and fully comprehend their loss, the treating physician pulled Regina aside and mentioned the possibility of organ donation. She wasn't sure how everyone would feel about that. She went back into the waiting room to discuss it with the family. She turned to the children first. Both were crying and obviously deeply grieved.

Finally, William answered first. "I think Dad would want us to do this."

Chloe agreed with her older brother. Whether the others really agreed or not, they outwardly supported the children's decision.

Over the next day, Jack was kept stabilized while the established system worked to match his organs with potential recipients. On Thursday, matches had been found for kidneys, liver, lungs, and heart. Surgeries were scheduled for Friday. That day, all the family arrived at the hospital early while the surgical team prepared to harvest Jack's organs for transplant.

When the time came to go to the operating room, the family was given a few minutes to tell Jack goodbye. Mary, Carol, and Tom went first. Carol and Tom told him he had been a great little brother, especially since his antics had kept the parents off their own backs. When it was her turn, Mary kissed Jack on the cheek and told him she loved him. She said he had remained her youngest because she had known it couldn't get any better after him. Then it was time for Regina, William, and Chloe to spend their last minutes with their husband and father. Chloe held one hand, and William held the other. Regina stroked his forehead and thanked him for being the best husband and dad she could have wished for. She kissed him for the last time, and medical personnel began to roll him away.

Usually, a family watches a loved one being taken to surgery with a great sense of hope—hope that the surgery will go well with no complications, hope that the medical problem, whatever it is, will be cured by the deft hands of the surgeons, hope for an improved life. Hope. For the family of an organ donor, the feeling is only one of despair and deep loss.

This is my commandment, that you love one another as I have loved you. Greater love has no one than this, than to lay down one's life for his friends.

—John 15:12–13 (NKJV)

30

THE GIFT OF LIFE

Jack was pushed down a hallway lined with hospital employees—a hospital tradition. All available employees would silently line the hallway as an organ donor was taken to surgery, to pay respects to the donor and the family. Regina, the kids, Marie, Carol, and Tom all followed Jack's bed. As Jack disappeared through a set of swinging doors to the operating room, Regina, William, and Chloe all broke down. All their hope was gone. They hugged. They cried. Regina said a short prayer for Jack and the intended organ recipients. And then they left the hospital to start a new life without him. At that moment, they were not comforted by the thought that their husband and dad would live on through the lives of the organ recipients. They just knew they would miss him.

Then shall the dust return to the earth
as it was, and the spirit shall return unto
God who gave it.
　　　　　　—Ecclesiastes 12:7 (KJV)

Most people on organ transplant lists had similar stories. Some had been healthy and then became sick. Others had been born with illnesses that caused their need for a transplant. Many of them hoped and prayed for a day that never came and then lost their battle to the illness that had landed them on the organ transplant list. The tragedy of Jack's death would give five people a second chance at life. Their hopes and prayers would be answered that day.

But those who hope in the Lord will renew their strength. They will soar on wings like eagles; they will run and not grow weary, they will walk and not be faint.
　　　　　　—Isaiah 40:31 (NIV)

But if we hope for what we do not yet have, we wait for it patiently.
　　　　　　—Romans 8:25 (NIV)

The kidneys are vital to life. They act as a filter to rid the body of waste and toxic substances, while returning vitamins, amino acids, glucose, hormones that help regulate blood pressure, and other vital substances into the bloodstream. Prior to receiving a transplant, people suffering from kidney disease often feel tired and weak and have trouble concentrating. Unfortunately, most kidney failure is permanent, and the patient's health will deteriorate over time. Once a person's kidney function drops to 10 percent or below, they must start dialysis, which performs the same function as the kidneys. Dialysis can be done in a hospital, in a clinic, or at home. The frequency and length of dialysis depend on the function of the actual kidneys, the size of the patient, the amount of waste and toxin buildup in the body, the amount of fluid weight gain, and the type of artificial kidney being used. Although each patient is different, the normal life expectancy of a person who requires dialysis is three to five years.

Once a person is on the kidney donor wait list, there is no way to know how long the wait will be. Most kidney recipients receive a kidney from a deceased donor, though a living person can also donate a kidney for transplant. The United Network for Organ Sharing maintains a list of all patients in the United States who need a kidney transplant. At any given time, that number is around 100,000 people. Unfortunately, the supply of organs from deceased donors can't match the number of needed kidneys. A living person can also donate a kidney since the body can function with just one. However, very few people volunteer to be a living donor, even though studies indicate that donating a kidney does not change a person's life expectancy. Most living-donor volunteers are family or friends of someone who needs a kidney transplant, but often the intended donor and recipient are not compatible due to various factors. In some cases, the National Kidney Registry can match up an incompatible donor-and-recipient pair with other incompatible donor-and-recipient pairs, resulting in two or more patients receiving a kidney transplant. This process is called a paired kidney exchange or kidney swap.

One of Jack's kidneys was transported to Louisville, Kentucky, for a forty-three-year-old woman named Susan. She had been undergoing dialysis for three years, but her condition was deteriorating quickly. Doctors estimated she had only a few weeks of life left. She had put her life on hold for the time she had been sick. After her successful transplant, she was inspired to become a nurse and enrolled in a local college program.

The other kidney went to New York City for Ken, a fifty-five-year-old police officer. Ken suffered from polycystic kidney disease (PKD), a genetic kidney disorder that eventually leads to kidney failure and the need for a transplant. He had struggled with PKD for fifteen years. He slept for ten hours a night but still would wake up feeling tired. About four years before, Ken's kidney function had dropped to about 10 percent, which had required him to start dialysis. By the time Jack's kidney arrived for transplant, Ken was using an at-home dialysis machine every day, sometimes at night, and even during his lunch hour when he could. He worked all he could, but he was chained to a desk and missed being on the streets. He had worked the same neighborhood in Brooklyn for thirteen years and had developed a reputation for being fair, helpful, and understanding. Make no mistake, he was a big guy and tough when he had to be. However, his philosophy was that building relationships within the neighborhoods was key to helping the people who lived there. He was a good cop, and the street missed him. Although he was popular with the people on his beat, no one had known he was sick until he had to take a desk job. After his transplant, Ken's energy level shot up, and he was eventually able to get back to his beat. He told his family and friends he had never realized how bad he had felt in the past until after his transplant.

Your liver helps fight infections and cleans your blood. It also helps digest food and stores energy for when you need it. A healthy liver has the amazing ability to grow back, or regenerate, when it is damaged. Anything that keeps your liver from doing its job— or from growing back after injury—can endanger your life. In the early stages of any liver disease, your liver may become inflamed, tender, and enlarged. Inflammation shows that your body is trying to fight an infection or heal an injury. But if the inflammation continues over time, it can start to damage your liver permanently. When most other parts of your body become inflamed, you can feel it—the area becomes hot and painful. But an inflamed liver may cause you no discomfort at all, and people with inflammation generally do not feel it. If your liver disease is diagnosed and treated successfully at this stage, the inflammation may go away.

If left untreated, the inflamed liver will start to scar. As excess scar tissue grows, it replaces healthy liver tissue, a process called fibrosis. Scar tissue cannot do the work that healthy liver tissue can. Moreover, scar tissue can keep blood from flowing through your liver. As more scar tissue builds up, your liver may not work as well as it once did. Or the healthy part of your liver has to work harder to make up for the scarred part. If your liver disease is diagnosed and treated successfully at this stage, there's still a chance that your liver can heal itself over time.

Cirrhosis is the scarring of the liver—hard scar tissue replaces soft healthy tissue. As cirrhosis becomes worse, the liver has less healthy tissue. If cirrhosis is not treated, the liver will fail and will not be able to work well or at all. Cirrhosis can lead to a number of complications, including liver cancer. In some people, the symptoms of cirrhosis may be the first signs of liver disease, including bleeding or bruising easily, water buildup in the legs and abdomen, jaundiced skin, intense skin itching, more sensitivity to medicines and their side effects, insulin resistance, and diabetes. Toxins can build up in the brain and cause lack of concentration, memory impairment, sleep issues, and other mental incapacities. Once you've been diagnosed with cirrhosis, treatment will focus on keeping your condition from getting worse. It may be possible to stop or slow the liver damage. It is important to protect the healthy liver tissue you have left.

End-stage liver disease includes a subgroup of patients with cirrhosis who have signs of decompensation that are generally irreversible with medical management other than transplant. Decompensation includes hepatic encephalopathy, variceal bleed, kidney impairment, ascites, and lung issues. The decompensated liver disease allows these patients to be prioritized on the transplant list.

Liver failure means that your liver is losing or has lost all of its function. When liver failure occurs as a result of cirrhosis, it usually means that the liver has been failing gradually for some time, possibly for years. This is called chronic liver failure or, again, end-stage liver disease. A liver transplant is required at this point. Liver transplant removes a diseased or injured liver from one person and replaces it with a whole liver or portion of a healthy liver from another person, called the donor. Since the liver is the only organ in the body able to regenerate, or grow back, a transplanted segment of a liver can grow to normal size within a few months. Often, transplanted livers are from people who were registered donors and who passed away. Since the liver has such regenerative ability, however, it is possible for a living person to donate a portion of his or her liver to someone in need of a transplant.

Jack's liver went to Knoxville, Tennessee. John was a high school music teacher in a small town in eastern Tennessee. He wasn't particularly popular with the students. They sensed that he was just going through the motions to get his paycheck and his retirement. They didn't know about his ongoing health issues, which were known only to family, close friends, and some colleagues. Like many patients needing a transplant, John was very private about his condition. He suffered from cirrhosis of the liver caused by nonalcoholic fatty liver disease. Most people think cirrhosis of the liver means a person was or is a heavy alcohol user, but that is not always true. Cirrhosis can be caused by excessive alcohol use, but there are other causes too, including hepatitis B or C. John suffered from the classic signs of liver disease, including bruising, water retention, a yellowish tint to his skin, and concentration issues. He had been waiting for a liver for almost three years, which meant he had lived longer than most people with liver failure.

The transplant saved and changed John's life. After he returned to school, his students found him to be an entirely different teacher—enthusiastic, engaging, and even inspirational. John's goal was for his students to appreciate and enjoy music. Anyone who visited his classroom would have said he met and far exceeded that goal. John's classes frequently resembled a party, with students singing, dancing, and just having fun. And of course, unbeknownst to them, the students actually learned something too. None of John's students went on to music careers, but a couple of them were inspired to pursue education careers and became teachers themselves. At his retirement ceremony, several former students showed up to show their appreciation for the positive impact he had made on their lives.

Cystic fibrosis (CF) is an inherited, chronic disease that interferes with the respiratory, digestive, and reproductive systems. Mutations of a specific gene affect the cells that line the organs of these three systems. This defective gene causes the production of thick, sticky mucus. It builds up and clogs the small airways and passageways that carry harmful bacteria out of the body. Because the bacteria is trapped, serious infections develop that weaken the organs and place constant stress on the immune system. Effective management of CF requires a variety of medications. Treatment regimens are demanding, and depending on the extent and severity of the disease, normal childhood activities are often disrupted by daily therapy and lengthy hospital admissions.

Rebecca was born with cystic fibrosis, and her twenty-five years of life had been a struggle. While some people don't show signs of CF until adulthood, Rebecca's symptoms showed at a young age. She had endured labored breathing, persistent coughs, poor weight gain, constant medication, and numerous trips to Shands Teaching Hospital in Gainesville, Florida. There is no known cure for CF. Like many CF patients, Rebecca would get to the point of needing a lung transplant.

At the time of Jack's accident, Rebecca was again a patient at Shands, but this time it was different. The life expectancy of a person with CF varies, with some people living well into their forties, but Rebecca's condition had worsened rapidly. On a Thursday morning, her doctors told her parents they should expect the worst for their daughter. Despite living with Rebecca's CF for many years and knowing this day could come, the family still felt like they had been hit by a load of bricks. When a loved one is sick, especially your child, you never give up hope, always praying for a miracle. Rebecca's parents and the rest of her family had always relied on their faith during difficult times. That day, they flooded Facebook with messages about Rebecca, asking all "prayer warriors" to hit their knees. By the end of the day, they learned that two lungs would be coming from Atlanta.

> Why, my soul, are you downcast? Why so disturbed within me? Put your hope in God, for I will yet praise him, my Savior and my God.
> —Psalm 42:11 (NIV)

Lung transplants are demanding physically and emotionally, with a slow and complicated recovery. Rebecca's surgery was successful, and she had a practically new life. She was able to do things that in the past had been impossible. She played with her son, learned to ride a bike, and went on walks with her mom. She lived life. She knew her life was still always at risk. Lung recipients must follow strict daily regimens to stay healthy—excellent hygiene, avoiding those who are sick, carefully cleaning food they eat, and use of immunosuppressive drugs that weaken the immune system. Lung transplant patients also may undergo pulmonary rehabilitation, physical therapy, blood tests, lung function testing, and more. The care lasts the rest of the patient's life. Lung transplants sometimes result in rejection, even many years later. Chronic rejection is diagnosed on average three years after lung transplant and can result in flu-like symptoms, including cough, chest pain, fatigue, fever, and shortness of breath.

Rebecca shrugged off all of the potential difficulties of her new lungs and poured her heart and soul into her family, her friends, and just living each day to the fullest. She also dedicated herself to helping other people with CF, giving them advice on how to cope with the disease, spending time with patients when she was at Shands, which was often, and being a beacon of hope for patients and their families.

31

MATTERS OF THE HEART

Jack's heart made the longest journey of all. The recipient was in Minneapolis, Minnesota. Rob was a local business owner who had gone from perfect health to needing a heart transplant in what seemed like a blink of an eye. Rob had grown up in a small town in Minnesota about a hundred miles from Minneapolis. In addition to being a good student, he was an avid hockey player and fan. He had learned to ice skate at a young age and started playing hockey when he was six. Like many hockey players, he had dreamed of a career in the National Hockey League. When it became obvious his talent couldn't get him to the NHL, he had enrolled at the University of Minnesota.

After college, Rob started working for an architectural firm and developed a specialty in medical facilities design. When he was thirty, he started his own firm with two other partners, each having their own specialty. Their business grew rapidly, and they were proud of their accomplishments. They treated their employees well, with competitive salaries, great benefits, and generous vacation allowances. All three valued their families greatly and wanted their employees to have plenty of time for their own families.

Rob had never made it past high school in hockey, but he still loved to play. Although he spent plenty of time with his wife and two daughters, Rob's one indulgence was Saturday morning hockey games with a group of men who called themselves the "NHL Could-Have-Beens." Rob rarely missed a Saturday. However, when Rob was forty-eight years old, he noticed he was getting tired much more easily. He also had some shortness of breath, weight gain, and lightheadedness. At first, he just thought it was a result of stress and getting older. He tried eating a better diet and exercising more. However, his symptoms got worse, and he finally went to his family doctor for a checkup. After an EKG and some other routine tests, Rob's physician referred him to a cardiologist. The cardiologist diagnosed Rob with dilated cardiomyopathy, which can be caused by coronary artery disease, thyroid disease, diabetes, viral heart infection, or heart valve abnormalities, among other things. Some people with the disease have only minor symptoms and live a normal life. Others aren't so lucky. Rob's heart disease progressed to the point that he would need a heart transplant. He was placed on the waiting list and could do nothing but hope.

By the time of Jack's accident, Rob and his family had practically given up hope. On two occasions, they had been teased with an available heart, but each time some problem had prevented the transplant from happening. When he was called to go to the hospital, Rob wasn't very optimistic. But this time was different. There were no problems. The heart arrived, and the delicate transplant surgery was successful. Jack's gift saved Rob's life.

When he returned to work, Rob proposed what seemed like a radical idea. He figured his partners would think he was crazy. They didn't. They embraced his idea, and it became company policy. From that day forward, 10 percent of all company profits was donated to charity. Each quarter, a different group of employees decided what charities would benefit from that quarter's profits.

32

ANOTHER GIFT

Regina's name and contact information had been shared with all the organ recipients. She had received very nice letters and a couple of Christmas cards, but that was all. In December 2016, she was very surprised when Rob called her

"Mrs. Hodges, this is Rob Glassman."

There was silence as Regina searched her mind for that name.

Before she could get out any words, Rob continued, "Your husband saved my life."

"I'm sorry, Rob. You caught me by surprise. It's wonderful to hear from you," replied Regina.

"I know this may be an imposition, and I will understand if the answer is no, but I'm going to be in Atlanta on business and would love to meet you and your family in person."

"I would love that," Regina said.

One evening during his trip, Rob went to the Hodges

home for dinner. They ate and swapped stories. Rob told them about his family and his business. Regina and the kids talked mostly about Jack and how proud he would be that Rob's business donated so much of its income to charity. After dinner, they went into the den. Rob was immediately drawn to the hockey stick, which was mounted over the fireplace. William and Chloe told Rob all about the stick, including the significance of the Bible verse.

"I'm home from the video store. Time for our movie!" Jack had yelled up the stairs.

At sixteen and eleven, the children weren't very excited about an evening in front of the television with their parents, but they had nowhere else to be and seemingly no way to get out of it.

Jack had rented the movie *Miracle*. It starred Kurt Russell as Herb Brooks, the coach of the 1980 US Olympic hockey team. The movie followed the trials and tribulations of the team, from tryouts through the Olympics, concluding with the gold medal ceremony in Lake Placid. Jack had told the kids about being at the game, and they knew he had the hockey stick in his office, but William and Chloe had never really understood how much the hockey stick meant to Jack. William and Chloe thought the movie would be rather lame, but they indulged Jack and Regina anyway.

When the movie was over, both of them said, "That was good, Dad," but their response lacked sincerity, and the two quickly escaped to their bedrooms. The story didn't mean much to someone who hadn't experienced the game live or even on television, and the kids soon forgot all about it—that is, until they lost their dad.

After Jack's death, the hockey stick was carefully placed in a spot where it was sure to be seen.

After hearing more about Jack, including his trip to Lake Placid, Rob told William and Chloe more about himself.

"I remember watching that hockey game between the US and the Soviet Union. I was about six years old. Right after that, I started playing hockey, and I've been playing ever since. When I was little, I wanted to play in the Olympics and get a gold medal, but my enthusiasm wasn't matched by talent."

William and Chloe both chuckled. "Do you still play?" asked Chloe.

"Yeah, I play most Saturdays with some other NHL wanted-to-be's," responded Rob with a slight laugh. "Most of us aren't very good, but we have fun."

William and Chloe looked at each other knowingly.

William leaned over to Chloe and whispered, "Are you thinking what I'm thinking?"

She was. They both thought their dad would want Rob to have the hockey stick. Regina had been listening to her children's conversation with Rob and nodded in agreement.

Rob resisted, but they wouldn't take no for an answer. He promised to take special care of it.

When Rob returned to Minneapolis, he mounted the hockey stick on a wall in the break room with a plaque beneath it.

Anything Is Possible
USA 4, USSR 3
Winter Olympic Games
Lake Placid, New York
February 22, 1980

33

DÉJÀ VU

In 2026, the Winter Olympics were set to return to Calgary, British Columbia, Canada. Rob had always wanted to go to the winter games and made plans to be there. The one event he really wanted to see was the gold medal game in hockey. The demand for tickets was great, but Rob was lucky enough to get two seats. One of his business partners, a former college hockey player, would join him. Over the past few Olympic games, a heated rivalry had formed between the US and Canada in hockey. The two teams seemed to always be competing against each other in the finals of big events. Canada had beaten the US in the 2022 Olympics, and the US had settled for the silver medal. Rob and Paul were hoping for a rematch and a different outcome.

As the Olympic tournament played out, there were some unexpected upsets, but in the end both the Canadian and American teams made it to the gold medal game. The game was set for a Saturday night and would be played in front of a packed house. Canadian fans were in the majority, but there were plenty of people dressed in red, white, and blue. Rob was wearing a red, white, and blue hockey jersey and carrying a hockey stick. That earned him a few odd looks and even some snickers, but he didn't care.

The game was close, just as everyone expected. At the end of the first period, the score was tied 2–2. The Canadians scored the only goal of the second period and led 3–2 going into the final twenty minutes. In the third period, the US began to control the game, outshooting the Canadians 8–1, but they couldn't seem to get that game-tying goal. With just over eight minutes to go, the US got a two-on-one fast break and put the puck into the back of the net for a tied score, 3–3. Then, with 2:58 left in the game, the US took its first lead with a goal scored off a rebounded shot. With two minutes to play, the Canadians pulled their goalie for a man advantage but couldn't manage to get off a clean shot. The US defense was just too strong and their will to win too great.

With ten seconds to go, the American fans counted down. "Ten, nine, eight, seven, six, five, four, three, two, one!" The buzzer sounded, and the Americans were gold medalists in hockey for the first time since 1980—USA 4, Canada 3. The American fans were going crazy. Strangers hugged and fist-bumped, and the older ones high-fived.

Rob and Paul were in the middle of the celebration, which included a little boy, about ten years old, wearing a US jersey. He had caught Rob's eye earlier in the evening; the boy was really into the game. Rob thought about Jack, Regina, William, and Chloe. He walked over to the boy and his father. He gave the dad a business card and then handed the hockey stick to the boy.

"I want your son to have this hockey stick," Rob said. "Call me and I'll tell you all about it." Rob figured this gift would have made Jack and his family smile.

Rob returned to his seat with an odd look on his face. Paul asked him if he was all right.

Rob replied, "I'm fine. I just had this weird feeling, kind of like déjà vu."

The feeling quickly passed, and Rob turned back to watch the US players still celebrating on the ice and to join in with the rest of the American fans.

"USA! USA! USA! USA!"

The End

LIST OF BIBLICAL
SCRIPTURES

Proverbs 19:17 (NIV)—Whoever is generous to the poor lends to the Lord, and He will repay them for what they have done.

Exodus 20:12 (NIV)—Honor your father and your mother, so that you may live long in the land the LORD your God is giving you.

Matthew 5:38–39 (NIV)—You have heard that it was said, "Eye for eye, and tooth for tooth." But I tell you, do not resist an evil person. If anyone slaps you on the right cheek, turn to them the other cheek also.

Matthew 6:24 (NIV)—No one can serve two masters. Either you will hate the one and love the other, or you will be devoted to the one and despise the other. You cannot serve both God and money.

Ecclesiastes 5:10 (ESV)—He who loves money will not be satisfied with money, nor he who loves wealth with his income; this is vanity.

Exodus 20:17 (NIV)—You shall not covet your neighbor's house. You shall not covet your neighbor's wife, or his male or female servant, his ox or his donkey, or anything that that belongs to your neighbor.

Proverbs 14:30 (NIV)—A heart at peace gives life to the body, but envy rots the bones.

Proverbs 22:6 (KJV)—Train up a child in the way he should go; and when he is old he will not depart from it.

Matthew 25:34–40 (NIV)—Then the King will say to those on his right, "Come, you who are blessed by my Father; take your inheritance, the kingdom prepared for you since the creation of the world. For I was hungry and you gave me something to eat, I was thirsty and you gave me something to drink, I was a stranger and you invited me in, I needed clothes and you clothed me, I was sick and you looked after me, I was in prison and you came to visit me." Then the righteous will answer him, "Lord, when did we see you hungry and feed you, or thirsty and give you something to drink? When did we see you a stranger and invite you in, or needing clothes and clothe you? When did we see you sick or in prison and go to visit you?" The King will reply, "Truly I tell you, whatever you did for one of the least of these brothers and sisters of mine, you did for me."

Luke 13:29–33 (NIV)—People will come from east and west and north and south, and will take their places at the feast in the kingdom of God.

Matthew 5:4 (NIV)—Blessed are those who mourn, for they shall be comforted.

Matthew 19:24 (KJV)—And again I say unto you, it is easier for a camel to go through the eye of a needle, than for a rich man to enter into the kingdom of God.

Matthew 16:26 (KJV)—For what is a man profited, if he shall gain the whole world, and lose his soul? Or what shall a man give in exchange for his soul?

Ezekiel 36:26 (NIV)—I will give you a new heart and put a new spirit in you; I will remove from you your heart of stone and give you a heart of flesh.

Matthew 6:3–4 (NIV)—But when you give to the needy, do not let your left hand know what your right hand is doing, so that your giving may be in secret. Then your Father, who sees what is done in secret, will reward you.

Romans 10:13 (NIV)—Everyone who calls on the name of the Lord will be saved.

Psalm 71:23 (KJV)—My lips shall greatly rejoice when I sing unto thee; and my soul, which thou hast redeemed.

John 15:12–13 (NKJV)—This is my commandment, that you love one another as I have loved you. Greater love has no one than this, than to lay down one's life for his friends.

Ecclesiastes 12:7 (KJV)—Then shall the dust return to the earth as it was, and the spirit shall return unto God who gave it.

Isaiah 40:31 (NIV)—But those who hope in the Lord will renew their strength. They will soar on wings like eagles; they will run and not grow weary, they will walk and not be faint.

Romans 8:25 (NIV)—But if we hope for what we do not yet have, we wait for it patiently.

Psalm 42:11 (NIV)—Why, my soul, are you downcast? Why so disturbed within me? Put your hope in God, for I will yet praise him, my Savior and my God.

Printed in the United States
by Baker & Taylor Publisher Services